"And you're t

Jamie plastered o... ...ce, but her knees were shaking. "Nice to meet you."

"Grayson Westler," he said and extended his hand. "Glad to see you in one piece."

"Guess my survival instincts kicked in." Jamie felt other instincts kicking in as she shook the hand Grayson offered her.

Grayson motioned her to a chair across from him. "Now, how can I help you?"

Jamie handed him a business card. "Well, as we discussed on the telephone last week, I'm a Realtor from the Whitestone Agency in Greenwich. I've come to discuss the proposal I put together to list your property."

"List my property?" Grayson frowned. "Hold on. Why do you think I'm interested in selling?"

The room seemed to grow hotter. "We discussed this last week on the phone," Jamie reminded him gently. "You said it was a great idea."

"I don't think we ever spoke on the phone," Grayson said.

Uh-oh. Jamie clutched her hands together. Was this some kind of cruel joke? Had she dialed the wrong number and spent an hour talking with some stranger with a very warped sense of humor? She groaned inwardly at the thought of all the personal questions she'd answered. "I spoke with someone who said his name was Mr. Westler. Not only that, but obviously my name was in your appointment book."

"Oh. You must have spoken with my father. He, well. . ." Grayson raked his fingers through his hair. "I'm sorry, but I'm not interested in selling. I'm afraid you've come all this way for nothing."

**KIM O'BRIEN** grew up in Bronxville, NY, with her family and many pets—fish, cats, dogs, gerbils, guinea pigs, parakeets, and even a big Thoroughbred horse named Pops. She worked for many years as a writer, editor, and speechwriter for IBM in New York. She holds a Master in Fine Arts in Writing from Sarah Lawrence College in Bronxville, NY and is active in the Fellowship Church. She lives in The Woodlands, TX, with her husband, two daughters, and, of course, pets.

Books by Kim O' Brien

**HEARTSONG PRESENTS**
HP641—The Pastor's Assignment
HP829—Leap of Faith
HP853—A Whole New Light

# A Still,
# Small Voice

*Kim O'Brien*

*Heartsong Presents*

*Special thanks to JoAnne Simmons, editor extraordinaire, for her unfailing encouragement and support. She's believed in me from day one, laughed at places in the book where I hoped she would, and gave me free rein to create. I am so thankful for you. I'm also very grateful to Rachel Overton and April Frazier for their excellent editorial work. They both worked tirelessly to bring the manuscript to the highest level possible. Additional thanks to the rest of the Barbour team who shepherded the book through its many stages of publication and distribution. You all are the best!*

A note from the author:
I love to hear from my readers! You may correspond with me by writing:

**Kim O'Brien**
**Author Relations**
**PO Box 721**
**Uhrichsville, OH 44683**

**ISBN 978-1-60260-625-8**

**A STILL, SMALL VOICE**

*Our mission is to publish and distribute inspirational products offering exceptional value and biblical encouragement to the masses.*

PRINTED IN THE U.S.A.

# one

"I'll think about it," Mrs. Madison said.

Jamie King kept her smile firmly in place. In real estate, a client saying, *I'll think about it,* was like a date going poorly and then ending with, *I'll call you.*

"What's the next house on the list?" Mrs. Madison flicked an invisible thread off the gray lapel of her jacket.

"There isn't anything else." Jamie kept smiling. "Have I mentioned the Brazilian cherry hardwood floors? The Viking appliances?"

During the past two weeks, Mrs. Madison had been inexhaustible in her quest for the perfect Connecticut home for herself and her husband, Fish, a retired Wall Street executive. They'd selected Greenwich—one of the most affluent and prestigious towns within commuting range of New York City—because Fish's best friend was a member of the Indian Harbor Yacht Club.

"Maybe we should go back to the little fixer-upper," stated Mrs. Madison.

The "little fixer-upper" was a 1.3 million dollar, 2,500-square-foot Cape Cod in Old Greenwich. "That one sold last week." Jamie placed her Realtor's card on top of the black granite countertop and gathered her car keys. Her feet ached in the darling but painfully high-heeled Ferragamo boots. She hadn't eaten since breakfast, and she felt the beginning of a headache. "I'll call you if a new listing comes available."

"Oh no," Mrs. Madison protested. "Fish will be so disappointed if I don't find something." She smiled, but there was a hard glint in her eye. "There's still a few hours of daylight.

5

Could we start from the beginning?"

It was dark by the time Jamie got back to her apartment building. She longed for a cup of chai tea as she walked across the marble foyer. She'd almost made it to the bank of elevators when she heard whistling coming from the mail alcove.

She stopped in her tracks. It was a little after five o'clock. Wilson never came this late. She looked around. There wasn't time to make a run for it. A moment later, the still-whistling mailman appeared around the corner.

"Oh good, Jamie," he greeted her. "Perfect timing. Your box is so full it's about to explode. Let me get your mail for you."

"Thanks, Wilson, but I'll get it later."

"Hold on a second—I've got my key right here."

Jamie shifted her weight and looked unhappily at the elevators. Avoiding the mailman and letting her mail accumulate—had it really come to this? She thought of her bills. Yeah, it had.

"Here you go." Wilson pressed a stack into her hands. She nearly groaned at the top letter staring at her—the one from Miss Porter's. Another notice about Ivy's unpaid tuition bill, no doubt.

"Thanks, Wilson. You take care. I think we're supposed to get some sleet tonight."

"Sure will. See you tomorrow."

Jamie stepped onto the elevator and pushed the button for the fifth floor. She'd have to call Ivy's school tomorrow and explain that she was waiting for a commission check. Miss Porter's wasn't the sort of boarding school for people who juggled bills and asked for payment extensions. Practically all the families who sent their children there had tons of money and social connections. Kids who graduated from Miss Porter's regularly went to Ivy League schools.

She'd have to juggle a couple of other bills and work out a payment plan with the school, then she'd call every client who'd ever expressed an interest in buying real estate. So what if December was the worst month of the year to be in real estate? She'd bring Jaya a box of Godiva, which might coax her into sending a few leads her way. She'd even venture into the morgue—the shelves in the basement filled with boxes of old, expired listings.

She'd been in tough times and gotten through. She would again.

◆

*Grayson Westler was fixing the split seat on the chairlift with duct tape when the call came. "Gray," his father's gravelly voice said through the receiver, "you better come straighten things out."*

The last time Gray had heard those words his dad had backed over the No Parking sign in the space between CVS and the Silver Shears beauty salon. The time before that, his father had taken out the landscaping in front of Talbots.

Gray gripped the cell phone tighter. "You're okay, right?"

"Oh yeah, but I need you to come get me."

"Where are you?" Gray was already walking to the parking lot, fumbling with his free hand for the keys to the Jeep.

"Danbury—at the movie theater," his dad stated matter-of-factly, as if he went there all the time. If you'd asked Gray an hour ago where his father was, Gray would have said he was in the ski shop sharpening the edges of the rental skis—not at the multiplex in Danbury.

The Jeep bounced over the washed-out ruts in the dirt parking lot. His father wouldn't even watch the DVDs Gray brought home from the video store. He always complained either there was too much violence or people were mumbling and he couldn't hear them.

Gray made the drive down I-84 West in record time. He didn't have a hard time finding his dad at the movie theater. The blinking red lights of twin security cars drew him like a beacon.

He found his father standing between two uniformed security guards. Something inside him relaxed slightly at the sight of his dad's familiar stooped frame and shiny bald head. "Dad!"

"Gray." His father's face relaxed for a moment, then tightened as he turned back to the security guards. "My son's here. Can I go now? Or are you going to arrest me? If you do, I'll warn you, I'm retired military. No jury in America would convict me. You'd end up looking like blooming idiots."

"Dad," Gray interrupted. "What's going on?"

"Your father hit two cars," one of the security officers replied. He had short black hair, chapped lips, and the blotchy complexion of someone who'd been standing in the cold for a long time. Chapped-lip Guy exchanged amused looks with the other guard. "We watched him do it."

The second security officer was a tall kid with a skinny goatee. "He backed into a car in one row, then hit the other one when he went forward."

"The spot was too small," his dad grumbled.

"When your father showed us his driver's license, we saw it had expired." Chapped-lip Guy gave Gray a sympathetic smile. "My uncle used to sneak out from the nursing home all the time, so I understand the situation. I told Norman here that if someone would come get him and he paid for the repairs to the other cars, we wouldn't make a big deal out of it."

"I am not feebleminded." His father's face flushed. "And I don't live in a nursing home."

"Dad." Gray shot his father a warning look. Arguing with the officer wouldn't make things any better. He turned to Chapped-lip Guy, who seemed more in charge. "That's nice of you," he said.

"We probably should wait for the drivers of both those cars to come out of the movies," his dad grumbled. "Give them our insurance information in person."

That could mean at least an hour. Gray checked his watch. Halle was due home at five o'clock. Rush hour was about to start, so if they didn't leave soon, he'd be late. He could text her—his daughter would rather give up oxygen than give up her cell phone—but he'd worry anyway. She was old enough to babysit, but he didn't think a thirteen-year-old should arrive home to a dark, empty house.

"How about we leave a note on the windshield with our phone number and insurance information?" Gray glanced at the bumper of a silver Volkswagen. It had a few scratches but nothing serious. Hopefully the car his dad had backed into also had minimal damage.

With the information exchanged, Gray and his father headed home. It started to rain as they pulled onto I-84. Gray's grip on the steering wheel tightened. Great. How was he supposed to make snow in this weather? Farther north, all this was probably snow. Mount Tom was opening next Saturday, and Killington, Stowe, and Mad River Glen had all been open since Thanksgiving. Not only that, but Mrs. Dodges, the woman who cooked breakfast for the B & B, had asked for time off to help a sick relative in Virginia. Finding a replacement on such short notice was going to be difficult. Plus, he'd have to ask Tony to drive back to Danbury with him tomorrow to retrieve his dad's car.

Next to him, his father misinterpreted Gray's silence. "I'm sorry," he mumbled.

Gray shot him a sideways look. "No big deal. But why were you here anyway?"

"To catch the four o'clock showing of *Sand-Castle Dreaming.*"

"A chick flick?"

"It had a good review."

"If you wanted to go to the movies, you should have told me. You don't have a valid driver's license."

"I would have my license," his dad pointed out, "if you would drive me to the motor vehicles department and let me get it renewed."

"And I would do that," Gray replied, "if I had any confidence that you wouldn't go around hitting other people's cars."

His father made a noise of disgust. "There's nothing wrong with my driving."

Gray pumped the brakes lightly as a car slipped into his lane. "Before I take you to the DMV, I want you to go to the optometrist and get your eyes checked. We'll get you a physical while we're at it."

"There's nothing wrong with my eyes or any other part of me."

"Please stop sneaking off in the car until we get you checked, and you've got to stop telling everyone you were in the military to get out of stuff."

"I *was* in the military," his father replied smugly. "Army reserves. And I was more than willing to go to Korea and fight for my country. I'd join the army today, if they'd take me. I could do it, too, Gray. I could drive a tank. You don't have to be young to drive a tank."

Gray squirted the windshield with fluid. The world blurred as the wipers swept across the glass. His father was winding up for his death speech—about how he didn't want to end up in a nursing home or attached to some machine in a hospital. He wanted to die while he was still useful. His dad would say that he would rather ski himself off a cliff than become a burden to Gray. He said this no matter how many times Gray tried to assure him it would never be like that.

Gray changed lanes as the traffic slowed. He could still make it back in time for Halle. He wouldn't meet her bus— she'd trained him not to do anything vaguely parental within sight of her peers—but he would have the house lights on and water heating for hot chocolate. He wondered how she'd done on her algebra test and if her friend Ella had been asked to the winter dance by Jackson Brennen, as Halle had been predicting would happen. He wondered if she'd have a lot of homework and if she'd worn the rain poncho he'd forced into her book bag early this morning. And he wondered when wondering about these things had become second nature to him.

## two

"Sorry baby," Jamie apologized as she eased her Lexus over yet another rut in what was more of a mud pit than a parking lot.

Welcome to Pilgrim's Peak.

She pushed her sunglasses into place and walked toward the gray, barnlike structure that crouched in the shadow of the mountains. Her gaze took in the blistered paint and the shingles peeling like a bad sunburn on the roof. The place looked in even worse condition than it had in the pictures she'd unearthed from the file in the morgue. No wonder Mr. Westler had sounded so eager to meet with her. He probably couldn't wait to unload the place.

She bought a weekend pass from a teenage girl at the lift ticket window and asked for directions to the bunny hill. She'd gotten the impression from Mr. Westler that he wouldn't even consider listing the place with someone who didn't love skiing. Jamie had never skied before, but hoped to impress Mr. Westler.

Sticking the lift ticket to the zipper of her new, fur-trimmed parka, Jamie hefted her skis—rented, but color coordinated with her parka—onto her left shoulder. They were awkward to carry and had been even more awkward to fit in her car, but she'd wanted to show up looking as if she were serious about skiing. The guy in the rental shop in Greenwich had promised these Rossignols would do it. As she followed a snow-crusted path to the other side of the building, she hoped he was right.

Pilgrim's Peak loomed in front of her, a tall mountain with trails of white cut through dense pines. A handful of skiers traversed a fairly steep pitch, moving slowly and gracefully. It didn't look that hard. The instructional video she'd rented also had been encouragingly simple. She'd watched Robert Redford in *Downhill Racer* for additional inspiration.

Sitting on the bench of a slightly wobbly picnic table, she put on her boots. They weighed a million pounds. As she lurched to her skis, she comforted herself with the thought that if she got this listing, she'd be able to pay off a lot of her bills and buy herself a pair of cute Manolo Blahniks.

Lurching her way across the snowy ground, Jamie headed for Looking Glass, also known as the bunny slope. She was panting by the time she reached it and paused to catch her breath. The slope was mostly scattered with small kids.

"Your first time on skis?"

Jamie looked down. A cute little girl in a pink ski suit stood next to her. "Yeah." Was it that obvious?

"Thought so." The girl turned to her equally miniature friend. "Better stand back. She looks like she's going to fall."

*Gee thanks.* Jamie watched the two of them slide past her, giggling as they effortlessly glided toward the chairlift—which wasn't a chairlift at all, but more of a towing machine.

Jamie was sure Robert Redford had sat down on his way to the top of the mountain. Probably this kind of lift was outdated and more evidence of the ski hill's financial fragility. She wished she had seen this on the Internet photos. She could have used it in her afternoon presentation.

Moving only slightly faster than a snail, Jamie covered the distance between herself and the antique-looking lift machine. Not only did it not have a comfortable chair to sit in, but it had a scary-looking J-shaped metal bar that went behind a skier's hips. The kids didn't seem to mind it, though. They rode stoically up the hill, their young faces comfortably blank like commuters on a train to Manhattan.

Jamie shuffled into the lift line. Before she knew it, the kid running the machine was yelling at her to hurry up and get in position. She tried, but her Frankenstein lurch wasn't fast enough and the boy ended up stopping the lift completely.

"Don't sit on the bar," the kid advised. "Just lean forward and let it push you up the hill. You ready?"

The little five-year-olds could do it, and so could she. Jamie nodded. The kid released her. The next thing she knew, she was getting an enormous shove in the rear end. She clutched the rope cable for dear life as the bar pushed her up the hill.

"That's good," the kid called after her. "Keep standing."

*This better be worth it.* She kept her gaze fixed on the munchkin in front of her and tried to keep her feet in the ruts made by the other skiers. She was doing pretty well, but then the J-bar slowed and the metal bar slipped to a spot above her knees. Before she could decide what to do about this, the machine started up again. The J-bar took out her knees, and Jamie fell. She slid on her stomach to the bottom of the hill.

On her next attempt to master the J-bar, she fell again. On her third try, she managed to catch the J-bar thing as she fell onto her stomach. Clutching it like a trapeze bar, she let it slowly drag her up the hill.

"Let go!" someone shouted.

Let go? Jamie grimly ignored the cold, mushy snow forcing its way down the neck of her parka. Her arms already ached, and she closed her eyes to concentrate better. It couldn't be that much farther to the top. She only hoped that her bindings wouldn't release before she got there.

The machine stopped completely, but Jamie wasn't fooled. It was crafty—and merely waiting for her to relax her death grip before it lurched forward. She set her jaw. The moment lengthened.

"You have to let go," someone was saying right in her ear. Jamie opened one eye. A gorgeous mountain man with dark brown eyes, shaggy brown hair, and a hint of razor stubble peered down at her.

Jamie opened the other eye. Mountain Man continued to loom over her, looking even more solid and mountainly now that she was looking at him with both eyes. He was smiling at her with very even, very white teeth. "It's not safe to let the machine drag you," he said. "You could twist a knee or something."

She shifted. Twisting a knee didn't sound very good, but neither did sliding to the bottom of the ski hill and having to start the whole process again. "I'll be fine. We're close to the top, right?"

"Not even halfway." His voice softened a little. "Let me help you."

"Just give me a second," Jamie said, trying to get a foothold with her skis. She didn't need help, even if it came from a cute ski instructor. That's what he had to be—his red jacket said SKI SCHOOL in lettering across his impressively broad chest. He had unbelievable eyes; the irises were a rich, chocolate color.

She might not need his help, but Jamie recognized the need to let go of the J-bar. The second she did, however, she began to slide. Mountain Man grabbed her hands before she slid out of his range. "I can do this," she insisted, trying to figure out how to stand up when she was still on her stomach and her skis prevented her from bringing her knees under her.

The next thing she knew, Mountain Man scooped her under the armpits and set her gently on her feet. "Maybe you don't need to go all the way to the top," Mountain Man stated tactfully. "Maybe you should try skiing to the bottom of the hill from this point."

Jamie brushed snow from the front of her coat and tried not to lose her balance in the process. She didn't want to seem helpless in front of Mountain Man, even if she was. "I'll be fine," she said.

"You know how to snowplow, right?"

"I've seen *Downhill Racer* twice."

He laughed. "That old classic? You might want to take some lessons."

"Maybe," Jamie agreed vaguely. She remembered the reason she'd come out to the hill in the first place—to gain information. "Have you worked here a long time?"

"Yeah." He glanced over his shoulder at a group of munchkins obviously waiting for him. "Look, I've got to get back to the ski school." He hesitated. "Make a big *V* with your skis—kind of like a pizza-slice shape. It's called a snowplow and will get you down the hill safely."

Jamie wished he'd asked her to go have a hot chocolate with him instead of giving her ski pointers, then gave herself a mental head smack. He was a thirty something ski instructor. Probably one of those guys who lived at home with his parents and wanted nothing more from life than a good pair of skis and a snowy mountain.

With a smile and a wave, Mountain Man skied off, effortlessly gliding across the trail. She watched him go until she was in danger of being caught looking at him, then began her snowplow to the bottom of the bunny slope.

## three

At 4:55 p.m. Jamie made her way down the long, narrow corridor that led to the ski hill's administrative offices. She paused in front of the door marked MANAGER to calm her heart, which was knocking so hard against her ribs she could barely hear herself think.

She smoothed her wool sweater over the black ski pants. Fortunately they seemed none the worse for wear after getting dragged up the bunny slope. She rapped her knuckles on the wood. *Be confident,* she ordered herself. *Smile like you're the most successful agent in Connecticut and people will believe it's true.*

"Come in," a deep voice said.

She lifted her chin a notch and stepped into the room. "Hello," Jamie said. "Thank you for meeting. . ." The rest of her sentence died on her lips. Mountain Man sat behind an oversized laminated desk cluttered with stacks of papers. He had on a pair of frameless reading glasses, and his brown hair looked comfortably rumpled as he stared back at her.

"You're Mr. Westler?" Jamie couldn't keep the surprise out of her voice.

"And you're the woman from the bunny slope."

Jamie plastered on the confident smile, but her knees were shaking. "Nice to meet you."

"Grayson Westler," he said and extended his hand. "Glad to see you in one piece."

"Guess my survival instincts kicked in." Jamie felt other instincts kicking in as she shook the hand Grayson offered her.

Grayson motioned her to a chair across from him. "Now, how can I help you?"

Jamie handed him a business card. "Well, as we discussed on

16

the telephone last week, I'm a Realtor from the Whitestone Agency in Greenwich. I've come to discuss the proposal I put together to list your property."

"List my property?" Grayson frowned. "Hold on. Why do you think I'm interested in selling?"

The room seemed to grow hotter. "We discussed this last week on the phone," Jamie reminded him gently. "You said it was a great idea."

"I don't think we ever spoke on the phone," Grayson said.

Uh-oh. Jamie clutched her hands together. Was this some kind of cruel joke? Had she dialed the wrong number and spent an hour talking with some stranger with a very warped sense of humor? She groaned inwardly at the thought of all the personal questions she'd answered. "I spoke with someone who said his name was Mr. Westler. Not only that, but obviously my name was in your appointment book."

"Oh. You must have spoken with my father. He, well. . ." Grayson raked his fingers through his hair. "I'm sorry, but I'm not interested in selling. I'm afraid you've come all this way for nothing."

Jamie's stomach gave an unhappy lurch. If she didn't get this listing, it was doubtful she'd be able to keep Ivy at Miss Porter's. *Forget Ivy's education,* she thought. *If you don't do something fast, you're going to be worrying about how to feed her.*

She pulled a slim portfolio out of her satchel. "Well, as long as I'm here, why don't I go over a few things with you?"

Grayson's dark brows pulled together. "I don't think that will be necessary."

Jamie's stomach tightened into a knot. Sometimes people said they weren't interested in selling, but they changed their minds when the price was right. "Well, it never hurts to know what your property is worth, does it?"

Grayson's voice grew colder. "I'm very aware of the value of this land."

"You've probably had a bank appraisal," Jamie argued. She

was practically steaming inside her wool ski sweater. "However, that's not the only value of your property. Given the location of your land and the growing market for people who want a rustic landscape, I estimate your land is worth. . ." She paused, then named a number. "That could be low. Condos are an option, too. Here, just look. . . ."

He shook his head. "You need to leave."

She was sweating harder now. "Your major competition is coming from Mount Southington and Otis Ridge. Both of these ski hills are within a thirty-minute drive of Pilgrim's Peak. Both of these hills have more trails, more uphill lift capacity, and more amenities. They market their hills with advertising campaigns and attractive, easy-to-use Web sites." Jamie paused. "I've done my homework, Mr. Westler, and everything I've learned tells me these other ski hills are attracting a lot more business than yours." She held his gaze despite the dark set to his jaw. "It's always better to choose to sell than be forced to sell."

"This meeting just ended."

Jamie figured she had about five seconds before he threw her out. "You'll be out of business in five years at the rate you're going. The table on page three shows inflation versus your business growth."

"Have a nice day." Grayson pointed toward the door with all the warmth of the Grim Reaper.

"Just think about it. . . ."

"I won't."

It was over. She saw it in his eyes. She stood slowly, burdened by the weight of failure that lay over her shoulders like a stone blanket. "You have my card." She paused at the door, trying not to hope for a last-minute miracle. "Thank you for your time."

She stepped into the hallway. A medium-sized man with a slightly stooped frame and glossy bald head was hovering nearby. "All things considered, that went pretty well," he said.

He followed her down the hallway. "Gray just has to get used to the idea. You can't change the brand of coffee you give him in the morning without hearing about it all day."

Jamie stopped walking. "Who are you?"

"Norman Westler." He extended a gnarled hand.

"Oh. You're the Mr. Westler who spoke to me on the phone."

"Call me Norman," the old guy said.

Jamie knew she should be irritated that Norman had led her on a wild-goose chase, but looking into his gentle brown eyes she just didn't have the heart. "Well, Norman," she said, "nice to meet you." She checked her watch and debated whether the traffic would be worse on the Merritt or I-95.

"You gave a very nice presentation," Norman said. "He shouldn't have cut you off like that. I'm going to have to talk to him about it."

"Oh, I'm used to it." Jamie decided to take Route 8 to the Merritt.

"I remember when we almost listed this place five years ago. A tall woman came here. She had big hair and an attitude—a real battle-ax. Her name was Theodora Roses."

"Oh—I know her. She's retired now," Jamie said.

Norman snorted. "Didn't like her much. But I give her credit," he said. "Must have come back here at least three times before Gray decided to let her draw up the paperwork." Behind his oversized glasses, his brown eyes looked at her intently. "My son is stubborn, but not stupid."

Jamie's eyes narrowed.

"He has a business degree from the University of Vermont. Graduated magna cum laude. You don't get that for your looks."

Jamie tapped her boot absently on the floor and ignored the voice that said she'd give Grayson Westler summa cum laude for looks. "So what are you saying?"

"Maybe you should stay a couple of days and work on him."

Norman held her gaze steadily. "I think with a little more encouragement he might come around. Personally, I'm ready to retire to Cape Canaveral in Florida."

Grayson Westler didn't seem like the kind of man who would change his mind easily, but something inside her was telling her to stay. *What do you have to go back to?* it argued. *An empty apartment and a stack of bills you can't pay?* Maybe it wouldn't hurt to give it another day. She'd packed an overnight case, and obviously this Norman guy was firmly on her side.

"So what do you think it would take," Jamie said slowly, "to change Grayson's mind?"

Norman smiled. "Well, for starters, I'd take some private lessons with him. That way you can get to know him a little better. He's not a bad guy."

Building a relationship made sense. "I could do that," Jamie agreed. "But I'd need a motel to stay overnight. Could you recommend one?"

"I can do better than that," Norman declared, positively beaming now. "You can stay with us right next door. Normally we don't open our B & B until next week—but as long as you don't mind roughing it a bit, I'd be glad to make an exception."

Jamie hoped he'd give her a good price, but was too proud to ask. She held out her hand. "Looks like we've got ourselves a deal."

≈

The wind gusted at the top of the mountain. Gray leaned his weight against the top of his ski boots and hoped the rest of the junior team would hurry. Evan, Christopher, and Derrick were already there, and he was impatient to start the practice.

"Hey, Mr. Westler," Whitney Clarke skied up to him, followed by Steffie Newbanks.

Gray hid his irritation as the minutes dragged past. He'd told Halle over and over that just because she had talent it didn't mean she could show up late at practice. Last year the junior ski team had come in dead last at all the club races, and this year everyone had agreed to try harder.

"Sorry, Dad," Halle's skis sprayed him with snow as she came to a clean swish-stop beside him. Ella, following, wasn't nearly as graceful and nearly plowed into Steffie.

Gray gave Halle a look that said he wasn't too happy with her late appearance. "Okay, everyone," he began. "Let's get started. We're working on carving turns today."

He gave the rest of the instructions and then skied to a good vantage point. The boys went first. Evan caught an edge on the first turn and wiped out. Christopher had technique but wasn't aggressive enough, and Derrick. . .well, Derrick stood at the top of the hill talking to the girls.

Gray had had this problem at the last practice. His junior ski team seemed to prefer talking to skiing. He briefly considered separating the boys from the girls, but knew he didn't have time to work with two groups.

Finally, Derrick pushed off with Steffie not too far behind him. Steffie had nice form, but lacked confidence. "Good job," he said as both kids slid to a stop beside him. "But bend your knees more."

"Thanks," Steffie mumbled, eyes on the ground.

Whitney went next, with Ella just a few turns behind. Gray made mental notes as behind them Halle started her descent.

His heart swelled up with pride at the sight of his daughter navigating the trail with sharp, clean turns. If only Lonna could see Halle now. Their daughter not only had inherited her thick, curly hair, but also her grace on skis. Lonna had sacrificed her skiing dreams when she became a mother. Gray intended to do everything he could to make sure Halle had the opportunity to go as far as her talent would take her.

A moment later, the kids clustered around him, their faces red-cheeked from cold. "That was good," he said. "But we can do better. All of you need to bend your knees more and use your edges. When we start doing slalom courses, it'll make the difference between making or missing a gate." He paused. "Got it?" He glanced at their faces. "Okay, let's finish the rest of this run and try it again."

He pushed off his skis just as Halle said, "Oh, Ella. Don't worry. Jackson will ask you. He's just waiting for the perfect moment. . . ."

Boys. Dating. Boyfriends. Gray skied the fall line along the edge of the trail. He and Lonna had been barely teenagers when they'd met, then the day she turned sixteen he asked her to the movies. He let his skis accelerate and felt the rush of cold air on his face. Neither of them had ever dated anyone else; they hadn't wanted to. He prayed Halle wouldn't follow in his and Lonna's footsteps—falling in love so young and then getting married before they finished college. While he wouldn't change anything about his life, he realized he wanted something different for his daughter.

*Please, God,* he prayed, *let her be a kid a little while longer.*

# four

Jamie signed the guest book at the registration desk. The B & B had potential—high ceilings, lots of interesting wood detail, and beautiful, although scarred, hardwood floors. But the house needed fresh paint, and there was a sizable chew hole in the red wool carpet in the foyer. The chewer of the hole soon became apparent as a golden retriever trotted down the stairs. The dog had a sock dangling from its mouth.

"Meet Boomer," Norman said. "Looks like he brought you a present."

Boomer pushed the soggy sock into her hands. Jamie wrinkled her nose and let the sock fall to the ground. Boomer immediately picked it up and patiently pushed it into her hands again.

"We're going to put you in the Duchess Room. It's on the second floor and has its own bath." He handed her the room key. "You might want to make sure you keep your door closed, otherwise Boomer will come inside and steal your underwear and socks."

"I'll be careful," Jamie promised. She followed Norman up the stairs to a door with the number two hanging crookedly on it.

"Dinner's at 7:30. I'm cooking spaghetti."

"Oh, I couldn't impose. . . ."

"It's no imposition." Norman winked. "Let's just say it's a chance to get to know each other better."

Translation: a marketing opportunity. Jamie relaxed. "In that case, I'd love to."

The Duchess Room featured a queen-sized brass bed that needed a good polishing, a maple dresser with a slightly cloudy

23

mirror, and a bookcase with an assortment of paperbacks. A tour of the bathroom netted a white-tiled floor, white fixtures, and a shower curtain with pictures of grinning Cheshire cats. Just what was it with all the *Alice in Wonderland* references?

The view from the room—the magnificent mountains, although too dark to properly admire—now *that* she could sell.

The house had not been included in the original listing, and she decided to factor it into a new proposal for Grayson, should he show any sign about changing his mind in selling.

Her cell phone rang. She smiled as she recognized the number. "Hey, Ivy, what's up?"

"Hi, Mom, guess what?"

"What?"

"Quinn Meyers invited me to spend Christmas break at their condo in Aspen!" The rapture in her daughter's voice came clearly through the receiver. "Can I go, Mom? Can I go with her?"

Jamie felt her palms start to sweat. A ski vacation sounded expensive. At the same time, she knew she had specifically chosen Miss Porter's so her daughter could develop social connections. "Absolutely. It sounds like fun."

"It's going to be so cool," Ivy enthused. "And she's only asking me. Not any of the other girls."

"Really? That's great, honey."

"We're going sleigh riding on Christmas Day, right after a huge brunch!"

It started to sink in that she and Ivy would not be spending Christmas together. She wanted to ask if Ivy had thought about this and decided she probably didn't want to know the answer.

"Quinn said to bring a bikini for the hot tub. My old one is kinda worn. Could I get another this weekend?"

Jamie sighed. "Of course."

"And could you call Mrs. Meyers tonight and let her know?"

"Sure." Jamie pressed the receiver more tightly to her ear.

"You doing okay otherwise?"

"Yeah. Look, Dara wants me to show her how to do this thing on her iPod. I gotta go."

"I love you, baby," Jamie whispered but wasn't sure Ivy heard. The phone already had gone dead in her hands.

❧

"You're doing really great, Halle." Gray pushed open the door and stepped into the welcoming heat of the house.

"The last run you had I timed you at just over a minute." He shrugged out of his jacket and bent to loosen the laces of his boots. "That's close to your best time, and the snow is pretty heavy."

Halle added her parka to the coatrack beside his. "I was thinking about my electives next year." She paused. "When I go to high school, I might want to take band. Ella says they need people to play the french horn."

Gray frowned. "I don't know, Halle. Our family isn't very musical." It hadn't been lost on him the way people turned around and looked at them in church when they sang.

"If I start taking lessons now," Halle said pleasantly, but firmly, "I might be able to play in the high school band. Ella's brother says sometimes they march beginner players if it's an instrument they really want in the show."

Gray rubbed his cold hands on his jeans. "I don't think you'll have time to do the ski team and something like band in high school." The pink bow of his daughter's mouth flattened with disappointment. "It doesn't mean no," he quickly added. "It just means we need to talk some more about this."

A clicking noise on the wooden steps caught his attention.

Boomer came clattering down the stairs, wagging his tail, a sock hanging from his mouth. "You stealing another one of my socks?" he asked fondly.

"Hey," a woman's voice said from the top of the stairs. That's mine."

Gray stiffened as he recognized the woman—the Realtor lady from Greenwich. The B & B wasn't even open for business yet. His gaze took in her heart-shaped face and very long, very straight brown hair. She held his gaze steadily. He remembered the kick in his stomach he'd felt when those big blue eyes had blinked up at him from the snowy tracks of the J-bar. He steeled his resolve as Realtor Lady trotted down the stairs.

"Thank you." She held the sock with clothespin fingers. "You stay out of my suitcase, Boomer." She didn't sound angry, though, and the golden thumped the floor with his tail and looked absurdly happy.

"What are you doing here?" Gray asked.

Her chin lifted a fraction. "Your father invited me."

"Who is she?" Halle asked, and Gray registered something like awe in her voice.

"Later, Halle," he said. He turned back to Realtor Lady. "We're not open to the public."

She smiled, oozing charm he would not let himself feel. "Norman already told me that. I don't need much—but if it's going to be too much of an inconvenience, I'll find another place."

Gray shifted his weight. He didn't want her staying with them, but Motel 9 was the closest place. He didn't like the idea of her staying there, either. However, if she as much as opened her mouth about selling Pilgrim's Peak, he'd drive her there himself. "You can stay, but don't expect the Ritz."

Her full lips formed an amused twist. "That shouldn't be too hard."

"Boomer, no!" Halle pulled back the golden just as Boomer started nosing the fringe on Realtor Lady's boots. "Go find a tennis ball," she said. The dog trotted off with his nose to the ground, tail wagging.

He realized introductions had to be made. "This is my daughter, Halle. Halle, this is Miss King."

Jamie gave Halle a warm smile and extended her hand.

"Please call me Jamie."

"Miss King," Gray corrected.

At five foot six, his daughter and Realtor Lady stood almost the same height. Something in his chest tightened as he watched his daughter staring at this woman as if she were a movie star.

"Is that a Juicy Couture charm bracelet?"

"Halle," Gray said in warning. He hated it when his daughter asked personal questions. And he wasn't exactly thrilled, either, that she was interested in Juicy Fruit—no, Juicy Couture—bracelets.

"Yes." Jamie smiled and held the bracelet up for closer examination.

"It's *so* cute."

He was spared any further conversation about jewelry as his father hollered, "Supper's ready!"

Inside the kitchen his dad was emptying a large pot of pasta into a colander in the kitchen sink. Wiping the steam from his glasses, he blinked at Gray in pleasure. "Ah, I see you've met our guest. Why don't you get Jamie something to drink with dinner, Gray?"

"Water's fine," Jamie said quickly. "I'll get it if you point me to the glasses."

"I've got it." Gray stepped toward the cabinets and pulled out the first glass he saw.

"You'd better make it a taller one," Halle said as Norman walked into the dining room with the bowl of pasta. "Grandpa's meatballs are usually pretty crunchy."

❧

The meatballs looked fine, but when she bit down on one, it was as hard as a golf ball. She slid it to the other side of her mouth and tried again with more force. It cracked open, spreading an unpleasant taste in her mouth. Jamie ignored Grayson's smirk as she washed it down with a long drink of water. Wiping her mouth with a napkin, she smiled at Norman. "Usually my dinner comes out of the microwave, so getting a home-cooked meal is a real treat."

She enjoyed the blush of pleasure that rose on Norman's cheeks and ignored the dark look Grayson shot her. She did, however, slip Boomer a meatball and hid the others in her napkin.

After dinner they cleaned up the dishes and walked into the family room. Norman settled into a leather recliner. Jamie sat on a plump, leather couch and picked up a skiing magazine.

Over the top of the page, she watched Gray crumple newspaper to start a fire in the stone fireplace. In front of her, Halle arranged an assortment of folders and textbooks on a badly scarred coffee table.

Jamie turned a page. Ivy had always taken her homework straight to her room. From an early age, she'd encouraged organization and independence. She heard the tear of a match and then the soft, whooshing noise as the crumpled newspaper caught flame in the fireplace.

"I have so much homework," Halle grumbled. "Want me to tell you what it is?"

Jamie set the magazine down. "Sure."

"Okay." Halle rattled off an impressive list.

"You're in public or private school?"

Halle snorted. "Public, of course."

"I thought only private school gave out so much work." Jamie stretched her tired legs toward the fire, which just now began to crackle. Behind her she could feel the cold December night seeping through the thick walls of the old house. "My daughter, Ivy, is in the eighth grade."

Grayson's head swung around. "You have a daughter?"

Instinctively she hid her left hand under the magazine so he wouldn't see the absence of a ring on her fourth finger. Despite the pride and love she felt for Ivy, she also felt the familiar stigma of the circumstances of her daughter's birth. "Yeah," she said, meeting his gaze. "She's at a boarding school in Farmington—Miss Porter's. It's a college prep school."

Halle and Grayson exchanged looks. Jamie couldn't tell if they were impressed with the school or slightly horrified that her daughter did not live with her.

"I've heard of it," Grayson said. "It's a great school."

An expensive one, too, which reminded Jamie of her need for a commission check. She shifted in the chair, wondering the best way to transition the subject from boarding school to her market analysis. "This is a nice house," she said casually. "How many square feet?"

"It's not for sale," Grayson replied firmly.

From the recliner, Norman's eyes popped open. "Maybe you should hear her out, Gray."

Grayson shook his head. "There's no need."

Norman's bushy eyebrows lifted. "I've been thinking about Cape Canaveral, Florida. I've been thinking it might be nice to live near the military base. Probably there wouldn't be so much driving I'd have to do."

"Is this what it's about, Dad? Your license renewal? Make the appointment with the doctor, and then we'll talk."

Norman's cheeks flushed. "There's nothing wrong with my eyes, ears, or anything else about me. I'm just saying, Gray, maybe you should hear her out. Hiding from the truth doesn't change things."

"The truth is we're fine." Grayson's jaw tightened further. "I have no interest in selling—today, tomorrow, or next year."

"She's right about the numbers. I was listening at the door, so I know what she said."

"You shouldn't be eavesdropping behind closed doors."

"I wouldn't have to eavesdrop if you'd leave the door open." Norman turned to Jamie. "I'd like to hear more about your daughter."

She blinked at the rapid change in topic. Why was Norman so interested in her daughter? She tried to read his face and was even more confused when he winked.

"What's she look like?" Norman prompted gently.

"Well," Jamie began. "She's about my height and has olive-colored skin and darker-colored hair."

"Is she in the band?" Halle asked.

"No. She's on the debate team and likes to ski." She saw the interest in Grayson's eyes. "She's an expert skier."

"Our school has this awesome band that goes to Carnegie Hall. You have to make Wind Ensemble, but by senior year, most kids make it."

"Homework, Halle," Grayson interrupted.

"Mrs. Hayes gives way too much algebra homework. I have, like, fifty problems—and she doesn't explain *anything*."

"Let me look." Grayson scooted next to her and bent over the math book, giving Jamie a nice view of his shaggy brown hair—all natural no doubt, no salon highlights and no hours of styling. "Okay," he said at last. "Look at the formula. $M$ equals $y_2$ minus $y_1$ divided by $x_2$ minus $x_1$."

"Huh? What's $M$?" Halle's nose wrinkled in confusion.

"The rate of change."

As Grayson started to explain, Jamie thought he might have been speaking another language. She was pretty sure they hadn't taught this advanced algebra when she went to eighth grade. And in high school, she'd barely gotten Cs in math. Of course, she'd been more interested in wondering if Devon Brown had noticed her new sweater, the way she was wearing her hair, her new shade of lip gloss—if he'd noticed anything about her. Anything at all.

Eager to escape these thoughts, Jamie settled back with the magazine. A short time later, she heard a very light popping noise, like a cork coming out of a bottle.

"Boom," Halle said. Hunching her shoulders, she pulled her turtleneck over her nose.

"Fire in the hole!" Norman yelled. He tucked his face into his red thermal shirt and looked braced, as if the ceiling were about to fall down on them.

Jamie was puzzled. Just as she turned to Grayson for an explanation, the most awful odor she had ever smelled permeated the room. "Ugh," she gasped involuntarily. Impossibly, it seemed to come in waves. She tried not to breathe, but could only hold her breath for so long. In his chair, Norman was shaking with laughter.

"Boomer." Grayson's voice was thick with disgust as he addressed the dog in front of the hearth. Looking up, he said, "Okay, who fed him the meatballs?"

Jamie raised her hand. "It was me. I didn't know."

"It's how Boomer got his name," Halle informed her happily. "If he eats anything besides his dog food, Boomer, well, *booms*."

"The silent ones are even worse. I'm thinking the military should study Boomer's gas," Norman commented, his voice muffled from under his shirt. "Drop a canister of that, and you'd have instant surrender."

"Enough, Dad," Grayson said in warning. "Come on, Boomer, let's put you outside for a moment." Grayson left the room with the dog at his side.

"How do you get your hair so straight, Miss King?" Halle asked when it was safe to come out from under her shirt. "I've tried to flatiron mine, but it never comes out very well."

"Well, tell me how you do it and what products you use." Before Jamie knew it, she was answering a multitude of hair and beauty questions and agreeing to straighten Halle's hair after the girl finished her homework.

Jamie didn't get to bed until late. Pulling the down comforter high under her chin, she tried to ignore the scratching noise coming from the vicinity of the closet. She really hoped whatever was making that noise wasn't chewing on her brandnew camel hair après ski boots.

Instead of the noise, she thought about Grayson and Halle crouched by the fireplace, their heads close together, their shoulders nearly touching. It was easy to see they had none of that awful awkwardness Jamie sometimes felt with Ivy. They probably never had that slight hesitation before they hugged each other to say hello or good-bye. She pulled the covers a little higher under her chin. Maybe it was different with fathers and daughters.

More scratching noises. Too loud to ignore. Jamie took a deep breath and fumbled with the light switch. She heard a low whine and realized she wasn't dealing with a mouse—and the sounds weren't coming from the closet, either. She exhaled, felt her teeth set in irritation, and marched to the bedroom door.

"Go away, mutt," she whispered. Boomer wagged his feathered tail hopefully. "I mean it," she said. The golden grinned up at her, deep kindness in his amber-colored eyes. Jamie had wanted a dog when she was growing up, but her mother had preferred cats. Her feet were freezing, and the dog wasn't going away, so she opened the door a little wider.

"Don't you dare steal my socks—or do any booming," she warned the golden, who trotted into the room and then bounded right onto the queen-sized bed. Jamie started to push the dog off the bed and realized she didn't have the heart. Besides, he'd make a great foot warmer.

The last thing she heard before she fell asleep was the dog's snoring blending with the odd creaks and wheezy groans of the old house.

*five*

Arriving early at the mountain the next morning, Jamie decided to take a couple of practice runs before her private lesson with Grayson. She braced herself for the J-bar's mighty shove and then remembered to lean forward and let the machine push her up the hill. She felt very accomplished when she reached the top without falling.

Norman had given her some pointers at breakfast, so when Jamie shuffled over to the beginning of the trail, she carefully arranged her legs into the snowplow position. *Keep pushing the backs of your skis apart*, Norman had coached, *and you'll be able to control your speed.*

He'd been exaggerating a bit about the control part, Jamie discovered a moment later. She was skiing down the mountain at a pretty good clip—but still standing—even though the snow was a lot lumpier than it looked. Then she saw the snaking line of the ski school just in front of her. "Look out!" she yelled.

The little kids didn't alter their course—or maybe they were like her, getting hijacked by their skis and couldn't. Jamie saw only one solution. She closed her eyes and threw her body to the side. Her bindings popped, and the next thing she knew, she was on her back and sliding headfirst down the mountain like a human torpedo.

She'd barely stopped sliding when Grayson loomed over her. "That was interesting."

"Interesting?" Jamie sputtered. She sat up and checked to see if everything still worked. "I almost kill myself, and you think it's *interesting*?"

"You look fine to me," Grayson said. "And at least you're near the bottom."

So she was—and it looked like the ski school was standing safely in line for the J-bar. Jamie took the hand he offered and let him help her to her feet.

"Guess our first lesson will be turning," Grayson said dryly.

Jamie thought the first lesson should be about empathy—his—then remembered he was a potential client. So, without any further comment, she followed Grayson to the J-bar. She made it to the top without an incident, and when she turned around to see if he was impressed, she nearly got hit by an empty J-bar swinging its way down the hill.

"You need to ski out of the path of the J-bar more quickly," Grayson lectured.

She had to bite her lip to refrain from telling him that getting knocked unconscious by the J-bar might be preferable to spending the next thirty minutes learning to ski.

"We need to work on your wedge turns," Grayson continued as they moved to the start of the trail. "I want you to follow me as closely as you can and copy my movements. Pay particular attention to the way I bend my knees into the turn and then straighten as I come out of it."

"Okay." Jamie flashed her best smile. "By the way, did you have a chance to look at that proposal I gave you last night?"

His lips tightened. "When are you going to accept that I don't intend to sell this place?"

"Your father and I had an interesting conversation at breakfast. He told me about this really great ski hill in Massachusetts that had been operating for thirty years—Powder Ridge—and then it had one bad year, 1995." Jamie paused to let this sink in. "It went into bankruptcy and was sold piecemeal at auction. I'm sure you don't want to see the same thing happen here."

Grayson shook his head. "It won't. I won't let it. Now, do you want to take this lesson or not?"

Jamie lifted her chin. "Yes."

Grayson pushed gently off the lip of the hill and began to glide down the mountain, making his movements slow and deliberate. Jamie set her jaw and followed. She'd been a cheer-leader in high school. Hopefully skiing was easier than making pyramids or doing a dozen back handsprings.

Grayson looked over his shoulder. "You're not following my turns," he pointed out. "You need to keep up with me."

She brought her skis together, sort of like the way Grayson was doing. Immediately she picked up speed. Grayson bent his knees, did some kind of tricky weight-shift thing, and turned. Jamie gamely bent, pushed hard on one ski, and twisted her body a little.

Grayson looked over his shoulder a second time. He nodded and picked up a little more speed. Jamie wasn't sure she could handle going any faster, but she wasn't about to ask him to slow down.

Her legs were shaking as she went into the next few turns. Surely he planned to stop and let her catch her breath. *And when he does,* she thought, *I'll hit him with a few numbers.* She hit a bump that Grayson had somehow missed. It put her off balance, and she missed a turn. She decided to let herself pick up speed so Grayson wouldn't lecture her about falling behind again. She pointed her skis downhill.

She let herself pick up a little too much speed, she realized moments later as she watched Gray's back rushing nearer and nearer. "Go faster," she yelled, but instead of immediately following her direction, he glanced back at her. She saw his mouth open in surprise, and then she slammed into him.

The next thing she knew, their skis tangled, and they were falling. She landed on top of him and heard his breath come out in a single whooshing noise, like a down cushion someone had sat upon too heavily. Her ski bindings didn't release, and when they finished sliding, she found herself on top of his chest with her knees bent and her skis sticking straight up in the air behind her.

He'd lost his hat and sunglasses in the fall, but at least he was breathing.

"Sorry," she whispered. "Are you okay?"

"I've been better." He shifted, but Jamie's skis, anchored in the snow, kept them both firmly in place.

Some of his shaggy brown hair had fallen across his face, and the rest was a tousled pile in need of a good smoothing. Jamie registered these facts, just as she registered that she'd tackled and squashed a potential client. "I don't suppose," she said slowly, "that now would be a good time to discuss my proposal?"

*⁂*

Jamie had always considered herself the kind of girl who made the best out of any situation. Trekking to the parking lot, she reviewed the positives of the past couple of days. She'd enjoyed meeting Norman and Halle, discovered that she liked skiing but really stunk at it, and had probably burned off enough calories in the past two days to fit into her favorite pair of skinny jeans.

She was still broke, of course, but she had the Coleman closing later in the afternoon, and while it wouldn't be enough to solve her financial dilemmas, it'd pay for Ivy's trip to Aspen. She'd juggle the rest of her bills. She was used to doing that.

She wasn't, however, used to losing her car. Frowning, she studied the place where she'd parked earlier that morning. There were track marks in the snow, but no cherry red Lexus. It wasn't anywhere else in the parking lot, either. Jamie nibbled her lower lip and rebalanced the skis currently digging into her right shoulder. Woodbury, Connecticut, didn't seem like the kind of place where people stole cars, but other than one other possibility—which her mind refused to accept—she couldn't figure out what had happened.

With her skis on her shoulder and her head held high, she marched back to the lodge area to straighten things out.

She found an empty picnic table near the concession stand. Two cups of coffee and several calls later, Jamie confirmed her worst fears—her Lexus had been repossessed. Not only that, but when she'd tried to rent a car, the credit company declined her charge card. She was trying to figure out what to do when her cell phone rang.

She recognized Marla Coleman's voice instantly and sat up straighter. "Mrs. Coleman. I was just about to call you."

"There's been a change of plans," Mrs. Coleman announced in the same girlishly happy voice that disguised an interior core of steel. "Geoff has been promoted to the London office."

"Promoted? London?" Jamie echoed but with far less enthusiasm. "What about the Hamilton Avenue house this afternoon?"

"Cancel it," Mrs. Coleman said.

"But your deposit. . ."

"There's the transfer clause, remember? We wrote it into the contract. In the case of an international transfer, our offer is rescinded in full."

A few minutes later Jamie hung up and replaced the cell phone in her purse. Her nose started to prickle painfully on the inside, the way it always did right before she cried. She dug her fingernails into the palm of her hand. *Don't panic,* she ordered herself and felt her body ignore the command as a sick feeling spread through her stomach.

Breathing shallowly seemed to help with the nausea, but didn't eliminate it completely. She dug her fingernails even harder into her palms. She'd figure out something. She always did. Maybe there was a bus she could take back to Greenwich and. . .and what? She swallowed something bitter tasting. How was she going to show houses without a car? She slammed her palm against the top of the picnic table. *You will not feel sorry for yourself,* she ordered. *You will not let this break you.*

Her nose positively burned now, and her eyes felt like they were floating in acid. She thought of Ivy, and her neck bent under the weight of despair. She laid her head on the flat surface of the table. It smelled like greasy french fries and ketchup.

"Miss King?"

It was Grayson Westler's voice. She tried to summon some last vestige of pride and sit up, but her head weighed too much.

"Go away," she muttered.

The table moved slightly under her cheek as he settled himself across from her. "What's wrong?"

"Nothing."

"Then why is your face plastered to the top of my picnic table?"

"Because I like it there," Jamie said.

"Are you hurt?"

"Nope," Jamie said, wishing it were that simple. "Just broke."

She sneaked a peak at him. He'd unzipped his ski instructor's jacket, and his impressive mountain-man chest was on full display. She had a feeling a girl could have a good cry on those broad shoulders. Not that she was that kind of girl. Nope. Jamie King was like the Lone Ranger. Only she wasn't the Lone Ranger—she didn't have a Tonto and her white horse had been led off to the repossession barn.

"Would you like me to call someone?"

Jamie straightened wearily. She really needed to pull herself together. "How about a cab?"

Grayson shook his head, then it seemed to register why she might be asking for transportation. "Did something happen to your car?"

"Repossessed." Normally she'd never have admitted that, but it occurred to her that once she got transportation, she'd never see him again. Therefore, for once, she didn't need to expend the energy to make it look like she had it all under control. "And don't ask me about leasing another car because I've maxed out my credit card. I just lost a sale that I've been counting on to pay my rent next month, and I have a daughter about to get out of school for Christmas break, and I'm not even sure how I'm going to *feed* her."

"Oh," Grayson said uncomfortably.

"I haven't spoken with my family in almost fourteen years, and if my friends find out I'm broke, I'm going to be professionally ruined." Her eyes began to tear, but it felt great to let it out. Why stop now? "Who wants to buy a house from an agent who has to borrow the client's car to drive to the showing?" She swiped her cheeks, angry at the tears for falling.

"You're that broke?"

"Yes." Jamie blew her nose into the tissue Grayson handed her.

He was silent for a long time. When he glanced up, he had an unhappy twist to his mouth and a fairly deep line between his brows. "Look," he said. "The lady who cooks breakfast for our guests has to take the next couple of weeks off for personal reasons. I'm looking for a temporary replacement."

Jamie blinked. "You are?"

"Our bed-and-breakfast opens next week, and we need a cook for the breakfast part. It's probably a bad idea," he added.

"No," Jamie corrected. "It's a great idea. I can cook."

"It doesn't pay much," Gray added.

"Just throw in room and meals," Jamie said, thinking rapidly. "And lift tickets." Ivy could spend Christmas break at Pilgrim's Peak instead of Aspen. "I'll need a car. To pick up my daughter from school and get a few things from my apartment."

"You'll need to be able to cook."

"I can cook." She saw doubt flicker across his eyes. "How about I make breakfast tomorrow? If you like it, you give me the job." She read resigned acceptance in his eyes. "And ski lessons." She held her breath. She probably shouldn't have asked for the lessons, but asking for a little too much was the way she negotiated real estate closings. *If you don't ask,* she always told her clients, *you'll never know.* "I make all kinds of breakfast pastries—and an excellent cheese frittata."

"Miss King, you've got yourself a deal."

"It's Jamie," she said, shaking his hand. "And thank you. You won't be sorry."

# six

Jamie went all out for breakfast. The day before she had checked the pantry. It was pretty well stocked. She was up before dawn and in the kitchen baking three kinds of muffins, frying up sausages, cooking hash browns, and making her specialty dish—an asparagus, tomato, and fontina cheese frittata.

She held her breath as she set plates down in front of Norman and Grayson in the dining room. Norman took one bite and began to laugh. It wasn't the reaction Jamie had been hoping for, and she felt herself start to sweat. But then Norman looked at her with a huge smile on his face. "I would never have thought someone as pretty as you could cook."

Jamie shrugged modestly. "My Aunt Bea taught me all her recipes." She glanced at Grayson, who was reaching for a second muffin.

"Who's Aunt Bea?" Grayson cut the warm muffin open and slathered it with butter.

Norman interrupted. "Whoever she is, she's a genius."

"She was a really good family friend," Jamie said. Normally she would never have mentioned Aunt Bea—or anything about that time in her life—but since Grayson was taking her in, she figured she owed him some information. "I lived in Maine with her during my senior year in high school. Want some more hash browns, Norman?"

"Absolutely." Norman held out his plate. "I'd love to meet your Aunt Bea. Is she single?"

She felt Grayson's gaze watching her carefully. His sharp brown eyes told her it would be difficult, if not impossible, to lie to him. Not that she was a liar, but Jamie disliked personal questions.

"Sorry, Norman, but she's been dead nearly fourteen years."

"That's too bad," Norman said very gently. "I'm sure she's in a better place now."

"I hope so." Jamie wiped an invisible spot on the table.

"So you grew up in Maine?" Gray asked.

Jamie's hands froze. "No. I'm from Connecticut. Darien, actually." She could feel his gaze trying to put the pieces of the puzzle together. She could have saved him the trouble and just told him the reason she'd been sent to the farthest corner of Maine was that her parents didn't know anyone in Siberia who would take in their unmarried, pregnant daughter. Instead, she met his gaze steadily. "So do I have the job?"

"Are you kidding?" Norman chuckled. "If I were a little younger, I'd be proposing marriage about now."

"Dad." Grayson said, warning in his voice. "Remarks like that are considered harassment."

"It's okay," Jamie said. She was sweating, but in relief. "So I have the job?"

Grayson nodded. "Just until Mrs. Dodges returns on January fifth."

*Perfect,* Jamie wanted to say, then thought of Ivy. School was letting out in a few days. "What about the car?"

"You can have Sally," Norman offered. "She's old, but she's like me—indestructible. You'll have to get the keys from my son, however." He shot Grayson a dark look. "He's hidden them from me."

"His license expired," Grayson explained.

"And *somebody* won't drive me to the motor vehicles department to get it renewed."

"I could drive you," Jamie offered.

Norman instantly said, "Great!" At the same time Grayson practically shouted, "No. And you know why, Dad."

Jamie held her hands up in surrender. "You two decide. I've got a lot of work to do." She had to let the office know she'd be away for several weeks. Plus she needed more clothing from her apartment and to have her mail stopped. There was grocery shopping to do, and Ivy to call.

Reaching for her cup of coffee, Jamie took a big swallow and felt the liquid burn its way down her throat. Ivy wasn't going to be happy about this change of plans, but hopefully she'd understand. Jamie would point out the positives. Being a Realtor had taught her that people, for the most part, didn't care if a house was perfect. They were willing to overlook a busy street or a backyard slightly too small if they could picture themselves doing something pleasant—like hosting football parties or throwing family barbecues. All they needed sometimes were a few prompts, and Jamie was only too happy to provide them.

&

Sally turned out to be a 1979 aquamarine Buick LeSabre. Its rust-stained body crouched as if sitting directly on its white-walled tires. The fenders were dented, and there was a fist-sized crack in the rear windshield covered with silver duct tape. "Isn't she a beauty?" Norman said proudly. "They don't make them like this anymore."

*And there's a reason for that,* Jamie thought as she squeezed the handle of the front door. It groaned, stuck, and then fell open at a funny angle. "What war did you say you drove this in?"

Norman laughed. He leaned through the driver's side window. "She likes oil, so when you get down to Greenwich, you might want to put a quart of 10W-30 in her."

Jamie nodded. She turned on the ignition. The engine whined, caught, and then the car backfired. Through the rearview mirror, she watched a cloud of black smoke wafting through the air. Norman was smiling like a benevolent parent, so apparently this was the norm. She shifted it into reverse. The car bucked so hard, she nearly hit her head on the steering wheel. Jamie set her jaw. A week ago she'd rather have died than be seen in a car like this one. Times changed, though. She wasn't exactly in a position to be choosy.

When she reached Miss Porter's, the only parking she could find was right in front of the quaint white Colonial-style house where Ivy lived. Heads turned as she pulled alongside the curb and parked next to a sleek black Lincoln Navigator.

Turning off the engine, Jamie braced herself as the engine went into the same theatrics as it had at her apartment—thumping, knocking, and emitting a sort of *ping-pong* sound under the hood. As the engine's gasps and coughs became more intermittent, she reached for her purse. With her head held high, Jamie marched up to the dormitory.

She found Ivy in her room, along with a small group of girls who were hugging and tearfully saying good-bye to each other. "Come on, Ivy," Jamie said, figuring she and Ivy should make a run for it before someone tried to tow old Sally to the junkyard.

Extracting Ivy from the dorm proved more difficult than Jamie had anticipated. Ivy's friends wouldn't let go of her, and they ended up following her to the car. All of them stood in the bright December sunshine staring at Sally's broad, rust-stained frame.

"Where's the Lexus?" Ivy asked.

"At the dealership, I think." Jamie opened the trunk and dumped Ivy's suitcase into the back. Standing on her tiptoes, she managed to clip Ivy's skis into the rack on top of the car. "You ready, Ivy?" She glanced over her shoulder at Ivy's friends and pulled out a megawatt smile. "You girls might want to stand back. Sally is a little temperamental."

She hustled Ivy into the car and started up Sally. The engine whined. Jamie gave it a little gas, and Sally backfired. The girls on the sidewalk gave a startled scream. Jamie shifted gears and braced herself for the forthcoming jolt. She ignored the startled look Ivy gave her. She also ignored the black cloud hanging in the air and the puddle of oil Sally left behind on the immaculate street.

"So," Jamie said brightly as they turned onto I-84 West.

"How does it feel to be on Christmas break?"

"Right now," Ivy said, "it feels like we're sitting right on the road."

"Sally rides low," Jamie agreed.

"I like the Lexus much better."

*Me, too,* Jamie thought. "You ready to do some skiing? The house where we're staying is right next to the hill." She glanced sideways at Ivy, trying to gauge her mood.

"My friends said that Pilgrim's Peak is a dinky little ski hill."

Jamie kept her gaze on the road. At least they were talking. "It is small, but quaint." Okay. Quaint was a stretch, but what was she supposed to say? "You'll like it."

Ivy snorted.

"So those looked like nice girls," Jamie ventured. "Which one was Quinn?"

"The one who's best friends with Dara now—because Dara is going to Aspen with her."

"Oh." Jamie tried to think of something positive to say. "Well, at least you and I will be together for Christmas."

"Yeah," Ivy agreed, but Jamie knew the word had been punctuated with an eye roll.

She didn't object when Ivy pulled out her iPod and ended the need for further conversation. She watched the gray landscape flash past and remembered the friends she'd had at Ivy's age. Most had been fellow cheerleaders. She remembered how hard it had been to fit in with them—she had to wear the right clothes and have perfect hair and makeup. She also had to be seen at the right places with the right friends. Jamie sighed, knowing she'd made Ivy look bad to her friends. She resolved to make it up to Ivy and buy her something really great the moment she had enough money.

About forty minutes later, Jamie turned off the highway. "Before we get to Pilgrim's Peak, there are some things you should probably know."

"What?"

"Take your earphones off." Jamie pantomimed the request.

"The house is a little run-down," she explained. "But it has a lot of character. The Westlers are nice people, and you are going to love the daughter—she's your age and is a really sweet girl." Jamie almost warned Ivy to be equally sweet, but then decided if she did, Ivy might do the exact opposite.

A short time later she pulled down the long driveway to the house. "We're here," Jamie announced unnecessarily and a bit too cheerfully.

"You're kidding." The sight of the old Victorian had temporarily snapped Ivy out of her campaign of silence. "Does it even have plumbing, or do I have to use an outhouse?"

Jamie laughed as if Ivy had been joking. "It has plumbing." She hesitated. "And Grayson's working on the hot-water problem."

"Seriously? No hot water?" Ivy's eyes widened with horror. Jamie clutched the wheel tighter and parked the Buick. They sat in silence as the engine refused to die and bucked liked a determined bronco.

"It has hot water," Jamie assured her. "You just have to shower fast."

"Why don't I just find a stream somewhere?"

Sally's last death rattle faded. "You could, but it'd probably be frozen."

Her humor fell flat. Jamie felt defeat, like the cold, seeping into the car. She steeled her resolve and wrestled open the door. She hauled Ivy's suitcase out of the trunk. She'd leave the skis for later. "Oh, one more thing. You know how I told you that you couldn't go to Colorado because one of my sales fell through?"

Ivy nodded.

"Well, this is sort of a working vacation for me. While I'm trying to get this listing, I'll also be cooking breakfast for everyone." Jamie climbed the porch steps. "Ivy, you coming?"

"Mom? You're working as a cook?"

"Don't look so shocked."

"But you don't cook."

How could Ivy not remember Jamie making her chocolate-chip pancakes—or blueberry crepes? *Because,* a voice inside said, *you decided about ten years ago that cooking didn't fit the image of a successful, professional woman.* "Don't be silly," Jamie scolded. "Of course I can cook."

They started up the steps. Ivy paused to stare at a Christmas decoration of a snowman on skis. Its hips were wiggling back and forth. "Mom," Ivy said. "Please pinch me so I can wake up."

Norman greeted them when they stepped inside the house. He shook Ivy's hand. "Gray's been making powder, and we've got twelve trails open."

After a brief hesitation, Ivy said, "Great."

Jamie shot her a warning glance. "You'll love the mountain, Ivy. It's right next door to the house. You can practically walk to the chairlift." She was babbling, but couldn't seem to help it. Ivy was making her nervous. What kind of mother got nervous around her own child?

Norman winked at Ivy. "Gray's going to let some moguls form on White Rabbit. You'll like them."

Ivy, to her credit, managed a strained but appropriate show of excitement. "Great!"

Jamie led Ivy upstairs. As they walked into the Duchess Room, Boomer followed them inside, a sock trailing from his mouth. "He's welcoming us," Jamie explained as Ivy uncomfortably backed away from the dog. Jamie took the soggy gift from Boomer's mouth into the bathroom and laid it on the side of the tub to dry.

When she walked back into the bedroom, Ivy was standing in the same place she'd left her. "Mom, there's only one bed in here."

Jamie nodded. "I know. We're sharing."

Ivy sighed. "This just gets better and better."

Jamie turned away so Ivy wouldn't read the disappointment in her face. Maybe she should have stayed in Greenwich in the silent apartment. They would have had their separate, tastefully furnished bedrooms and wouldn't have to interact so much. It would have been a lot easier to pretend that everything was right between them.

## seven

After the Westlers returned from church the next morning, Norman invited Jamie and Ivy to help pick out their Christmas tree. Jamie put down her shopping list. "Thanks, Norman, but we wouldn't want to intrude on your family time."

"Intrude?" Norman laughed. "You can referee." His gaze moved to Ivy, who was sitting on the sofa in front of the fireplace reading *The Call of the Wild*, or at least pretending to. Jamie hadn't seen her turn the page in the last five minutes. "Hey, Ivy," he said. "Ever cut down your Christmas tree?"

The girl lowered the book. "No. We have an artificial one."

"That's not a tree," Norman scoffed. "That's a coatrack." He stepped closer to her. "I'll show you a real Christmas tree. Get your coat."

"It's actually kind of fun picking it out," Halle added. She was eyeing Ivy's striped cashmere sweater appreciatively. "Dragging it home isn't so much fun."

"You drag it home? The store is that close?"

Norman laughed. "The store is in our backyard, Ivy. Just look out the window."

"And it's starting to snow!" Halle cried. She whipped out her cell phone and blasted off a text.

True enough, outside the glass fat white flakes were gently falling. Jamie wanted her daughter to participate, but feared anything she said would make Ivy do the exact opposite. She didn't think their relationship had been this bad at Thanksgiving. Looking back, Jamie realized they hadn't spent much quality time together. Ivy had slept late and then spent hours texting her friends.

"What do you say?" Norman pressed. "You want to go hunt

for the perfect Christmas tree?"

Ivy looked less bored than before. She put aside the book.

"I guess."

Within minutes, Ivy and Jamie retrieved their coats and boots and joined the Westlers in the backyard. Grayson was wearing a black parka and carrying a rusty-looking saw in his hands.

"That saw looks serious," Jamie said as they all marched off across the frozen field. "The last time I bought a Christmas tree all I brought along was a charge card."

Grayson shot a glance at his father. "Don't think we can buy the kind of tree we're looking for."

"That's true," Norman agreed.

Ivy and Halle ran ahead. Boomer raced alongside, his golden coat already dotted with snow. When Jamie was little, her mother had told her that in every snowfall there was always one flake that tasted as sweet as sugar. If she ever caught this flake on her tongue, she could wish for whatever she wanted.

"Did you ever catch one?" Jamie had asked, completely buying the story, just as she'd accepted the existence of Santa Claus and the Easter Bunny.

"Oh yes," her mother had said. "Just once, though."

"And what did you wish for?"

Jamie remembered her mother's blue eyes resting on her, warm as a summer sky. "I wished for you," she'd said.

Jamie thought of this story every time it snowed. Even though it also made her a little sad, she'd told this story when Ivy was very little. In Jamie's version, Ivy was the child who had been wished for.

"Just what kind of tree are we looking for?" Jamie asked, picturing the towering, lush blue spruce her parents had always placed in the marble foyer.

"We'll know it when we see it," Grayson said cryptically.

"The girls are having fun together," Norman remarked. "It's nice for Halle to have Ivy's company. Usually it's just us old farts and her."

"Speak for yourself," Grayson said mildly.

Jamie admired their easy bantering. She and her parents had never teased each other the way Grayson and Norman did— and she didn't do it with Ivy, either. She was always afraid Ivy would take what she said in a bad light and get her feelings hurt. Probably it was a guy thing, not something she had failed to do as a mom.

The woods were getting thicker now. They were almost at the base of the hills. Dozens of fragrant pines mixed with the skeletal limbs of hardwoods. Jamie spotted a tall, elegant tree with thick boughs. "How about that one?"

Grayson barely gave it a glance. "Nope."

"What about it don't you like?"

"Not enough personality," he replied.

"What do you mean, personality?" Jamie pushed aside a branch and crunched over the frozen ground after Grayson.

She couldn't help but feel that finding the right tree was a lot like finding the right house for a client. The better she understood the criteria, the easier it was to find the right match.

"Kind of hard to define," Grayson replied.

They tracked deeper into a cluster of pines. The snow was definitely sticking now. The trees already had a light dusting, and the vast gray sky seemed to hang right over them, looking like it was capable of snowing for days. In the distance the girls held out their arms and spun in the thickening fall of snow.

"Your daughter is lovely," Grayson commented.

Jamie glanced at him suspiciously. "Thank you."

"I was impressed to see her doing some homework this morning. She must be an excellent student."

Jamie wondered where the conversation was going. "She works hard for her grades."

"So does Halle," Grayson said. "But not on the second day of Christmas break." He laughed lightly as if this were amusing.

"Well, it's the exam schedule," Jamie said vaguely. "Ivy has four finals waiting for her after the break. I guess it's a good thing she didn't get to go to Aspen."

"She was going to Aspen?" They walked a few more steps. "Is that where her dad lives?"

So this was where the conversation was going. Jamie planted her feet. She waited until she had Grayson's gaze firmly locked within her own. "One of Ivy's friends from her school invited her," she said in a frosty tone. "Her dad isn't in the picture."

Jamie felt her cheeks heat as Grayson studied her face. She braced herself for further questions, but none came.

"Dad! Over here!"

Grayson turned at the sound of his daughter's voice. Jamie followed more slowly. She kind of wished she hadn't been so prickly. He'd invited her—a total stranger—into his home.

No wonder he was trying to understand her situation. She shouldn't have gone off like that.

When she caught up, Ivy and Halle were standing next to a skinny pine tree with a hook-shaped tip.

"I like it," Norman stated. "A tree with osteoporosis. Sort of like me."

Grayson tested the strength of the trunk. "It has potential, but let's keep looking."

Halle and Ivy ran deeper into the trees. Norman followed at a much slower pace and Boomer happily dragged a branch through the woods. Jamie ducked under a branch and stepped over some deadfall. "So you're looking for deformed trees?"

"We like to think of them as unique."

Jamie still didn't understand. "Why choose an ugly tree when there're so many beautiful ones all around?"

Grayson's boots crunched as he headed toward another smaller pine. "Not ugly, Jamie. Our trees have personality. And it's a family tradition. How do you and Ivy pick out your tree?"

"We go to the basement and bring the box to my apartment." It was a nice tree, a four-foot-tall blue spruce, perfectly shaped and prelit with perfectly spaced white lights. "We decorate it with red balls and sterling silver ornaments." Actually, Jamie was the only one who decorated it. Sometimes Ivy helped, but afterward Jamie would have to rearrange the decorations into a neat, symmetrical look.

"I'm sure it's very nice." He said it tactfully, but Jamie could tell he didn't think that at all.

"It is," she stated firmly.

From up ahead, Halle shouted, "We found it! Dad, come look!"

Halle, Ivy, and Norman stood in front of a medium-sized tree. At first Jamie didn't see what was so special about it, but then Norman moved to the side and she saw the center branch sticking out at least a foot longer than any of the others.

"It has a nose!" Halle cried. Out came her cell phone, and she snapped a photo. "See it?"

Grayson smiled. "It has definite personality. What do you think, Dad?"

"I like it," Norman said. He seemed a little out of breath and rubbed his arm as if it hurt.

"You okay, Norman?" Jamie moved closer to him.

"Oh sure," he said. "Old army wound. Got it in the Korean War. I drove a tank, you know."

"Dad," Grayson said. "I don't think they had tanks at Fort Myers, Florida."

Norman straightened as much as his bent frame would allow. "How do you think they train people to drive tanks, Gray? You think they just ship them off to war with a set of tank keys and say 'good luck'?"

"I'm just surprised I hadn't heard about you driving tanks at Fort Myers before," Grayson said.

"Well maybe I just don't like to go around bragging," Norman said. His breath came out in small white puffs, and he rubbed his arm again. "You don't know everything about my life."

"I want to hear more about the tanks," Ivy said, surprising

Jamie with her show of interest and support. "How do you see where you're going?"

"A very good question," Norman said approvingly. "There's a little window with metal slats, just like in a knight's helmet. You can close the opening if someone shoots at you."

Grayson's eyes narrowed suspiciously. "You sure, Dad?"

"Absolutely," Norman said, meeting his gaze.

Grayson shook his head as if he didn't quite believe him, then stepped close to the base of the tree.

Jamie watched Grayson's arm move back and forth and listened to the metal teeth slice through the wood. Suddenly she was seventeen years old, seven months pregnant, and using a steak knife to saw a bough off the pine in Aunt Bea's backyard. The smell of sap was strong, and she remembered sawing and sawing until her fingers went numb and the ache of cold spread up her fingers. She hadn't let herself quit, though. She wasn't about to let her baby spend its first Christmas without a tree, and Aunt Bea was too old and too sick to go out and get one.

She'd stuck the branch in a glass vase, decorated it with tin-foil balls, and put it on the coffee table in front of the fireplace. She remembered sitting on Aunt Bea's cat-smelly couch and wrapping her arms around her swollen stomach. *Don't worry, baby,* she thought. *I'm going to take great care of you. And next year we're going to have a real Christmas, with lots of presents and a beautiful tree with red balls and sterling silver decorations. I'm going to love you more than any kid in the world, and you're going to have a great life. I promise.*

# eight

It would have been a lot easier just to drag the tree home himself, Gray decided as they neared the house. He held the base, Jamie and Ivy the front, and his dad and Halle had the middle. Every time they had to go around something, Jamie and Ivy would try to go different directions, then argue which way made more sense. If this wasn't bad enough, Norman complained nonstop that everyone was walking too fast, and Boomer kept trying to play tug-of-war with the branches. And then, when they were almost home, Halle realized she'd dropped her cell phone somewhere along the way, and they all had to go back and look for it.

Gray was relieved to get the tree home and into the family room. He was even more relieved when the fat trunk fit into the old metal stand.

"Let's put giant sunglasses on him," Halle said. "That'd look so cool."

"Him?" Gray turned the screws that held the tree in the base. "How do you know the tree is male?"

"Because he has a moustache," Halle said, shaking the pine bough of the limb that stuck out of the middle of the tree. "See, the pine needles are like whiskers."

"Hold on, Halle, it isn't properly secured." Gray gave the bolt a final twist and straightened. The tree fit perfectly into the corner of the family room. "Trees aren't girls or guys, they're just trees." He tested the trunk to make sure it was balanced. Out of the corner of his eye, he saw Ivy watching. She was a pretty girl, but all too often he'd noticed a petulant look around her mouth, especially whenever she addressed her mother. He wondered what sort of mother/daughter team he'd brought into the house—and if hiring Jamie King was going to turn out to be the worst mistake he'd made in a long time.

It was only for a couple of weeks, he reminded himself as he opened the plastic storage box and pulled out a strand of globe lights. Besides, he sympathized with her financial problems. He'd had a couple of bad years where he'd wondered if he was going to be able to hang on. Always God had provided, and the help had come in many forms. In all good conscience, he could not have turned Jamie King away.

"Anyone want some hot chocolate?" Norman asked.

"Me," Halle said.

"Me, too," Ivy chimed in.

"Then you'd better come help me make it," his dad said. "You know I can burn anything."

"That's true," Halle said. "One time he even burned cereal."

"It was oatmeal, Halle," Norman said, chuckling as if he was proud of the accomplishment. The three of them disappeared into the kitchen.

"You want some help?" Jamie stepped over Boomer, who was chewing a bone in his usual spot on the hearth rug.

"Sure." Gray climbed up on a chair and clipped the first bulb to the top of the tree. He handed the string of lights to Jamie, who wound it around the other side of the tree. He secured these lights, too. "You know the Madisons, Fieros, and Kemplers are checking in tomorrow afternoon, right?"

"Yes," Jamie said.

As Gray handed her the light strand, he brushed her skin by accident. A small, electric thrill moved through his fingertips. It was gone as quickly as it happened, and he told himself it had been nothing more than static electricity.

He'd dated other women since Lonna died, but there'd been a flatness to the whole experience he'd found discouraging. He'd taken them to dinner, movies, walks through the shops in town. Although he could find nothing wrong with the women, he always felt as if he were just going through the motions of dating. Part of him wasn't quite there.

"Breakfast starts at six a.m.," Gray stated, careful not to let their hands touch when the strands came back to him.

"Don't worry," Jamie flashed a bright smile up at him. "I'm doing raisin scones with honey butter, scrambled eggs with chives, and Canadian bacon—kind of a run-through for when the guests arrive."

"Maybe you should be in the restaurant business instead of real estate."

Jamie laughed. "As long as we only serve breakfast." She fished another set of lights from the storage bin and handed him the end. "Besides, I love being in real estate. Even though it doesn't seem like it right now, I'm really pretty good at it."

He stepped off the chair and passed her the string of lights. "You been doing it long?"

"For thirteen years," Jamie said, hooking lights along the branches in the back of the tree. "I started as a receptionist and worked my way up."

He couldn't help but do some mental math. That put her somewhere between thirty-one and thirty-five. Looking at her smooth, clear skin and long, glossy hair, he would have guessed her age to be younger than that.

"I was ten when I started," Jamie said and then laughed. "I'm kidding. I was eighteen."

"That's pretty young." Thirteen years. He did more calculations. She'd had a job and a baby. He wondered how she'd managed both. When he'd been eighteen, he was a freshman at college, dating Lonna, and working on a business degree. His most consuming thought—besides Lonna, of course—had been how to go even faster on the downhill racecourse at Stowe.

"How about you?" Jamie retrieved the smaller, twinkler lights from the box and handed them to him. "When did you start running Pilgrim's Peak?"

"Oh, pretty much right after college." He reached the pro-truding branch. It already had been wrapped with the red globe lights. "You think we should add more lights to Pinocchio's nose?"

Jamie put her hands on her hips and regarded the tree. "Better not. It might start to droop." She looped the strands around the lower branches. "You didn't consider doing anything else? Not that running Pilgrim's Peak isn't a great job."

Gray hesitated. Running Pilgrim's Peak, in truth, hadn't been his life's ambition. "Oh, for a while I thought about a racing career. I had some sponsors lined up, but then it just worked out better for me to come back to Pilgrim's Peak." The lights were finished now, but he made no move to step away from the tree and neither did Jamie.

"What happened, Grayson?"

Her eyes were soft and gentle on him. She had a beautiful face, but it was not her beauty that made it hard for him to look away from her. He sensed something fragile about her, a brokenness that she worked hard to hide. He would not have recognized it if it were not something he had seen in his own mirror.

"I got married my senior year in college. And then we had Halle." He paused. "When you have a baby, it changes everything."

&

*A baby changes everything.* The words echoed in Jamie's mind. She was glad when Norman, Halle, and Ivy carried a tray of hot drinks into the room. She took a hot mug and walked to a solitary spot by a large, frost-framed window.

She looked at the falling snow but saw the parking lot of the Darien YMCA. It was a warm May night, and Devon had just finished working out. They were holding hands, and he was asking her if she wanted to get a burger at McDonald's. She looked up at his perfect face and knew she couldn't put it off any longer. "Devon," she said. "I have to tell you something." She took a breath. "We're going to have a baby."

She flinched as his fingers tightened painfully around hers.

"What did you say?"

She tried to smile and felt the muscles in her cheek quiver. "I'm pregnant."

He let go of her hands to rub his face firmly, as he always did when he was thinking hard. She dug her fingernails into her palms and prayed that when he opened his mouth he'd say something about them being in this together.

"Are you sure?"

Jamie nodded.

"I'm eighteen years old," Devon said, "and leaving for Ohio State in a couple of months. I don't want to be a father." He drew his hand through the thick, dark hair she'd admired so often. "How do I even know it's mine?" He'd looked at her so coldly she'd actually shivered. "This changes everything, Jamie."

And it had.

# nine

The guests couldn't check in before four o'clock. This gave Jamie almost an entire free day. She decided to spend as much of it as possible with Ivy. By ten o'clock they were in line at the double chairlift. She was a little nervous. Grayson had promised to teach her how to get on and off the lift, but he hadn't had time. She didn't want to embarrass herself in front of Ivy.

When it was their turn, Jamie skied into position. Just like Ivy, she watched over her shoulder as the chair came nearer and nearer. The attendant steadied it, but somehow it knocked into the back of her legs anyway. Jamie sat down with a *whoosh*, and then the chair rapidly propelled them upward.

"Mom," Ivy said. "Are you okay?" She pulled the safety bar into place.

"Yeah," Jamie replied, watching the ground get farther and farther away. "So, tell me about school. How's algebra going?"

"Good."

"And your English class?"

"Language arts. Good."

"And history. It's world geography, right?"

"It's US history, but, Mom, you don't have to pretend you're interested." Ivy studied the ground.

"But I *am* interested. Look, I know you're upset with me about the Aspen trip. Trust me, if I could have afforded to send you, I would have."

This earned her a snort of disbelief. "You bought a new jacket and skis. There was enough money for that."

Jamie sucked in the cold air. She glanced at Ivy. How could a kid change so much in the space of a few months? And yet was it such a big change—or had she simply been closing her eyes for a long time and thinking that Ivy's snarky remarks and disrespectful attitude were just part of teenage angst?

"The skis and boots are rented. The jacket is new, but honey, when you're a real estate agent, you're not just selling property—you're selling yourself. You have to look right if you want people to take you seriously. Appearances matter."

Ivy made a snort that definitely wasn't agreement.

Jamie expelled a long, frosty plume. "People judge you by how you look. You know I'm right."

Ivy lapsed into silence. It grew steadily colder as they climbed the mountain. A sign attached to a rocky part of the cliff read PREPARE TO UNLOAD. At this point Jamie thought she might be ready to jump right out of the chair. She hated that things between her and Ivy felt so broken. Didn't Ivy know that everything Jamie did in her life was for her?

Ivy lifted up the safety bar. Jamie's stomach started a free fall at the sight of the open air below her. Beside her, Ivy wiggled forward on the seat, and the chair lowered as Jamie's skis bumped down onto the snowy platform.

Standing, Ivy used her free hand to push herself away from the moving chair. Too late, Jamie realized she should do the same. The chair swung around the corner with Jamie still sitting on it. "Stop," she yelled.

A teenage boy with a bad case of acne stuck his head out of a hut on the platform. "Um, you okay?" he said.

"Yes," Jamie replied. "Can you back this thing up?" She glimpsed Ivy hightailing it down the trail underneath the lift line.

"Sorry," the kid said. "You'll have to ride the chairlift back down the hill."

Jamie started to argue and realized it would be pointless. She pulled the bar back into place and tried to ignore all the perplexed looks from people whom she passed on their way *up* the mountain. Finally, about six minutes later, she reached the base of the mountain and began the trip back to the top.

This time the minute Jamie's skis touched the snowy platform, she gave herself a mighty shove off the seat. Unfortunately, it sent her to the far edge of the ice-coated ramp. She panicked and crossed her ski tips. She crashed and took several people down with her.

"Sorry," Jamie apologized, trying to crawl out of the pileup but hampered by her skis, which were tangled with another skier's. She got her legs under her as a boy on a snowboard slid down the ramp just inches from her nose.

"Stop the lift," a familiar voice ordered.

As Jamie struggled to her feet, another skier knocked into her from behind. She felt the breath rush out of her as she was propelled forward. She rammed straight into Grayson, who caught her just before she crumpled. "Nice running into you," he said.

Jamie extracted herself from his grasp. She tried to come up with a snappy retort, but the best she could do was say, "Oh, Grayson, is everybody okay?"

"Everybody's fine." He smiled, and Jamie felt her heartbeat pick up speed. There was just something irresistible about him—like a big piece of red velvet cake with gobs of rich vanilla frosting. She knew it wasn't good for her, but it was impossible to look at it without wanting it.

"I have to find Ivy," she said, firmly ordering her thoughts to more acceptable channels. "You haven't seen her, have you?" She pointed to the nearest trail. "I saw her going down that one."

Grayson frowned. "That's White Rabbit. I don't want you taking that trail. I've let some moguls form on it."

So that's what you called those lumpy things that from the chairlift made the trail look like the surface of the moon. She'd probably kill herself—or someone else—if she tried that trail. By now Ivy probably was waiting at the base lodge for Jamie anyway. She sighed. "What's with all the *Alice in Wonderland* names?"

Grayson chuckled. "It was my dad's idea. My mom's name was Alice, and he wanted to honor her by naming all the trails after characters in the Lewis Carroll novel."

"That's so sweet," Jamie said, genuinely touched. She could easily picture Norman being that kind of a romantic. "Well, then," she said. "If you'll just point me to an easier trail, I'll be on my way."

"I don't like the idea of you taking your first run down a novice trail by yourself."

"In our last lesson you said I was ready for novice trails," Jamie reminded him.

"Hey, Dad!" Halle called, skiing up to them. "We're tired of waiting. You coming? Oh hi, Miss King."

Gray addressed his daughter. "You all go ahead. I'm going to see Miss King safely down the mountain."

"I'm fine," Jamie tried to wave him off. "Don't worry about me."

"Halle, please tell the others to take a warm-up run on Alice's Alley and then meet at the double chairlift in twenty minutes."

"Gray, seriously. I don't need a babysitter."

"It's a safety issue."

"You help everyone down the mountain their first time?"

"When I see someone who needs it, yes."

Her chin came up a notch. "And you think I'm one of those people?"

"Most people don't have trouble getting off the chairlift."

He had a point, so Jamie stopped arguing. He brought her to a trail called the Queen of Hearts. It wasn't nearly as wide as the Looking Glass, and it was steeper. She could barely control her speed and once or twice came perilously close to skiing into the pines. However, as Gray coached her from behind, they progressed farther and farther down the trail.

At one point, the trail leveled slightly, and she was able to enjoy the scent of the peppermint air and the sensation of gliding through the silent pines. She thought of Gray skiing behind her. In her mind he was Gray now—not Grayson Westler, the owner of the ski hill. Grayson was much too formal a name for a guy like Gray. Gray ate muffins in two bites and had eyes that could either be dark as coffee or light as amber. Gray radiated some vibe that made it impossible for him to go anywhere on the hill without at least a dozen kids chasing after him.

He also had a past which she knew nothing about. He had a child but wore no wedding ring. Wouldn't it be ironic, Jamie wondered, if it turned out that he had a life story similar to hers?

*Skkkkkkk.* The ice hissed under her feet. Suddenly Jamie's skis swung around like windshield wipers. She was on the ground in an eyeblink. Her bindings released, and her skis chased her down the slope. Grayson was at her side in a flash. "You okay?" His brown eyes assessed the situation.

Jamie lumbered to her feet and brushed the snow off her parka. "Yeah. I lost concentration for a moment."

He handed over her ski poles and one of her skis. The other had slid a little farther down the hill. Jamie was about to go and retrieve it when a skier flashed past. Jamie recognized the black and neon blue ski suit.

"Hey!" Gray yelled at the skier's rapidly retreating back. "Slow down!" He shook his head. "Some of these kids," he muttered, "have no clue how dangerous it is to bomb the hill like that. If I see that girl again, I'm giving her a warning. And if she does it again, I'll pull her ticket."

Jamie laughed without humor. "That kid was my daughter."

Gray's eyebrows pushed together. "Your daughter skis like that?"

"When she's trying to avoid me," Jamie said dryly.

Immediately she wished the words back. It made Ivy look bad in his eyes. He was probably judging her daughter, which was totally unfair. He had no clue about Ivy—how hard it had been for Ivy to grow up with no family other than Jamie. What it felt like to be rejected before Ivy was old enough to know what the word meant.

"She's probably just letting off some steam," Jamie added quickly. "Miss Porter's is a tough academic school, and Ivy is a straight-A student."

"You've got to tell her to slow down. If she runs into somebody going that fast, she could seriously hurt them."

Jamie nodded. "If it helps, she knows what she's doing."

"She looks like she's had some good training," Gray admitted.

Jamie felt herself relax slightly. "She has. Gary Blanco—up at Killington." It had cost a cool fortune, but Ivy's best friend's family had a condo there and she'd been invited to go nearly every weekend. Jamie made sure Ivy had gotten the best lessons and skied on the best equipment possible.

"Why didn't you take any lessons?"

Jamie shrugged. "Weekends are busy when you're a realtor." Besides, there hadn't been enough money. More than once she'd stretched a box of macaroni and cheese because she couldn't afford anything else. But he didn't have to know that.

She wanted him to see her North Face ski jacket, the half-karat studs in her ears, the side-swept bangs that were the perfect length and style. She didn't want him to see the caramel highlights in her hair that needed a touch-up or know that the skis and boots were rented. She didn't want him looking too deeply into her eyes, either.

If you hid your flaws well enough, she'd learned, you could almost forget they existed at all.

# ten

Gray got Jamie safely down the rest of the trail. She wouldn't promise to stay on Looking Glass, which he would have liked, but there wasn't much he could do about that. Besides, plenty of beginners skied the intermediate trails, he reminded himself. She'd be fine. Still, he felt uneasy and promised himself to keep an eye out for her.

The juniors were waiting for him, per his request, at the double chairlift. He noticed Ivy standing beside Halle.

Gray skied up to them. "You want to ski with us, Ivy? We're going to run some gates on Alice's Alley."

"Is it a black diamond trail?"

"It's an intermediate trail, but if you want to ski fast, you need to do it with us."

Ivy shrugged and looked bored. "I guess."

A short time later, they were standing at the top of Alice's Alley. "Okay," Gray began. "We need to get ready for the first club race, which is only two weeks away. I've set a slalom course. You've skied one before, haven't you, Ivy?"

"It doesn't matter if you haven't," Ella said. "Most of us aren't very good." She shot Halle an apologetic glance. "Except for Halle."

"You're all good skiers," Gray said.

"Last year we came in dead last out of five teams." Whitney giggled as if this were funny.

"I had a bad knee, man," Derrick said.

"This year will be different," Gray promised. The skepticism remained on their faces. Gray couldn't really blame them. The other ski clubs had the benefit of starting their training earlier and having longer courses to practice on. They had larger pools of talent to pick from as well. "Okay. Keep the green gates on your left and the red gates on your right. Who wants to go first?"

Ivy raised her hand. Gray skied the course first. When he reached the finish line, he waved his hand to indicate he was ready. Ivy swung herself forward, and he clicked the stopwatch.

He'd known she was fast, but he wanted to see if she could turn. From the moment he saw her swing through the first gate he knew she was good. So good, in fact, he almost forgot to click the stopwatch when she sped past him.

Ivy's time, it turned out, was a half second better than Halle's. He was still thinking about it at the end of the afternoon when he walked into the ski shop. A half second was a lot of time. Ivy was on better ski equipment than Halle. A new pair of racing Rossignols would make a great Christmas present for Halle. Until then, he'd try changing the kind of wax on the bottom of Halle's skis. His dad might have some thoughts on that.

His dad was bent over the worktable, sharpening the edges of a pair of rental skis when he walked into the room. To his surprise, he saw Jamie working at the counter. She was laughing with a customer who was returning a pair of ski boots.

He walked over to her. "What are you doing?"

"I was taking a break from skiing and saw that Norman could use a little help." She began wiping down the countertops with a bottle of window cleaner. "I saw Ivy come down the hill with Halle. Thanks for including her."

"You shouldn't be behind the counter," Gray said. "It's for employees only."

"Oh, don't be stodgy," Norman said. "She's doing a fine job. Tell us about Ivy. She gonna join the junior ski team? You could use her, Gray. Last year we took a lot of ribbing for coming in last place."

Gray shrugged. "Ivy is welcome to join our team or just ski with us."

Jamie smiled. "I'm sure she'll be excited to be on the team." Her brows drew together. "But you'd better be the one to ask her, not me."

He nodded. "We ran some gates, and she had the fastest time." Gray found himself staring at the bare spot on the fourth finger of Jamie's left hand. He thought about his gold wedding band, carefully packed away in a box in the top drawer of his dresser, and wondered if she had a similar ring packed away. If she'd ever held it up to the light and looked through the opening at a future that no longer existed.

"Glad all those lessons paid off," Jamie said.

"It's more than lessons," Gray admitted. "It's God-given talent."

A mother and two sons walked to the counter to return their rental equipment. Out of curiosity he watched Jamie interact with them. She smiled a lot. And her brown hair was long, very straight, and shiny.

"And don't forget, if you're here, to join us for the Christmas Eve Torchlight Parade," Jamie told the family. "Every year on Christmas Eve Pilgrim's Peak offers free lift service to the top of the mountain. There's a brief nondenominational service at the trailhead, then everyone turns on their flashlight and skis to the bottom of the hill. Afterward, there's hot chocolate and doughnuts in the lodge."

The family asked to sign up. Gray turned to his dad. "How does she know about the Torchlight Parade?"

"I told her, sonny boy," his father replied happily. "She's been signing people up like crazy. I think we're getting more teenage boys than we've ever had. They take one look at her and get a glazed look in their eyes—sort of like the one you just had on your face."

"I did not," Gray stated firmly, but his dad only laughed.

❧

Jamie and Ivy drove old Sally the short distance back to the B & B. "So," Jamie began as the car bounced slowly down the rutted driveway. "Did you have fun today? I heard you were the star of the Pilgrim's Peak junior ski team."

Ivy was busy texting. When she finished, she looked up and said, "What?"

Jamie repeated her comment.

"Oh." Ivy studied the keypad on her phone. "That isn't saying much."

"Well, did you have fun?"

"It was okay." Ivy's phone buzzed, signaling the arrival of a text message. This time Jamie waited until after Ivy had sent the message to speak.

"I'm sorry we didn't get to ski together," Jamie added, hoping Ivy would apologize for ditching her, but not being entirely surprised when her daughter's only response was the irritating clicking noise of her phone as she texted.

"How long are you going to do this, Ivy? Be angry at me?" Jamie turned onto the main road and then immediately put on her turn signal. "Because, frankly, it's getting a little boring."

Ivy sat in stony silence.

Jamie's gloved hands tightened on the wheel. "Say something. Argue with me. Agree with me. Just don't sit there like a bump on a log." Too late, Jamie recognized the phrase as one her mother had often used.

"Okay. What do you want me to say?"

"Who are you talking to? What are you saying?" Jamie tried not to sound as desperate as she felt.

"I'm talking to Quinn in Aspen."

"What's she saying?"

Silence.

Jamie pulled old Sally into a spot in front of the big Victorian. As the engine began its death throes, she studied the dark curtain of her daughter's hair. It was a few shades darker than her own, much closer to Devon's color. Ivy had his square jaw, too. Not that Ivy knew either of these things. Devon had been very clear that he wanted no part of Ivy's life, and Jamie didn't want to say or do anything that might encourage Ivy to seek him out.

Ivy concentrated fiercely on texting a message—likely something about her loser mom. Jamie wanted to reach across the bench seat, grab the cell phone, and throw it out the window. She imagined herself hugging her daughter until something in Ivy broke and she hugged Jamie back.

Jamie tapped the wheel instead and wondered how Gray would have handled this situation. Impossible to know. Halle was so sweet. Jamie couldn't imagine the curly haired brunette giving Gray a hard time about anything. If Halle had been in Ivy's position, she would have pitched in and helped with Jamie's chores. Why didn't Ivy?

Maybe because Jamie wasn't a very good parent. Her stomach clenched as she considered the possibility. She thought of the sacrifices she'd made and shook her head. No. It was a teenage thing, something that Ivy would outgrow. Her grip on the steering wheel eased.

Maybe if she pretended not to notice Ivy's sullenness, she wouldn't be reinforcing the behavior, and it would simply go away. She checked her hair in the rearview mirror and freshened her lipstick. Guests were due soon, and she wanted to make a good impression. "You ready to go inside?" She didn't expect a response, and she didn't get one.

# eleven

"Dad," Halle said as she and Gray walked into the kitchen the next morning. "There's only fifteen hours left on the auction, and the bidding is still at a hundred dollars. The french horn is worth triple that."

Jamie was at the kitchen sink and up to her elbows in sudsy water as Gray and Halle walked into the room with their breakfast dishes. She was scrubbing an omelet pan and trying to remember if Aunt Bea had used vanilla or almond extract in the white chocolate drizzle she planned to use to top the raspberry scones the next morning.

"Hey, Jamie," Gray said. "Excellent breakfast."

She flashed him a grin. "Thanks."

"Dad," Halle said. "You want me to place a bid for you?"

"Halle," Gray said patiently. "How do you know the instrument is really as good as it seems? Buying something off the Internet sounds risky."

"Ella asked her brother to ask the band director to look at it. Dr. D said he knew the company selling it, and it's a good one."

Gray set his dish on the counter. "Wouldn't you rather have new skis?" Jamie smiled at the hopeful note in his voice. "There's a new generation of racing Rossignols that's just coming out."

"My old ones are just fine," Halle said. Jamie heard the firm but polite note in the girl's voice. She'd make a great real estate agent—relentless but polite. "Dad, I won't give up skiing, but I really want to do band. Ella's brother is going on a really cool trip to New York City."

"Taking cool trips is not a reason for wanting to join the

band." Gray gave Jamie a look that said, *Help me.* Reaching for a dish towel, he began drying the omelet pan. "If you're on the ski team, you'll go to lots of really cool places. When your mother was in high school, she was the Eastern High School girls' giant slalom champion." He paused. "You're just as good, if not better, than she was."

Jamie accidentally shot herself with water from the sink hose at the mention of Halle's mother.

"I know, Dad," Halle said. A note of resignation crept into her voice. "It's just that band sounds like fun."

Jamie handed another soaking-wet dish to Gray. "Band does sound fun," she said. "The kids in band at my high school always looked like they were having a great time." She ignored the look of warning in Gray's eyes. "They rehearsed like crazy. Nobody worked harder than they did, but you could tell they all knew and liked each other."

"That's what I heard." Halle flashed a grateful smile at Jamie. "Were you, like, in the color guard or something?"

"A cheerleader," Jamie admitted.

Gray set the skillet in a drawer. "I'm sure band is a lot of fun, but, Halle, I want you to think about what you're giving up, really think about it, and pray about it before you make up your mind. Now, if you want a ride to the hill with me, you'd better go and get ready. I've got a nine o'clock lesson."

After Halle was out of earshot, Jamie turned off the faucet and wiped her hands on a dish towel. She felt like the last person on earth who should be giving parental advice, but something inside prompted her to speak. "You really want her to ski, don't you?"

"She's good." Gray refilled his coffee cup and leaned against the counter. "I don't think she understands just how good she is or what it could mean to her future."

Jamie nodded. "Maybe she'd be great in band, too."

"Unfortunately, tone deafness runs in the family. Things might not work out the way Halle thinks they will."

Jamie picked up a rag and began to wipe down the counter. "Things usually don't work out the way you think they will." Case in point: Look where she'd ended up.

"I know," Gray replied. "But I have the perspective of being a lot older. I'd hate to see her throw her talent away."

Jamie thought of the countless times she thought she'd known what was best for Ivy. She was beginning to understand, though, that enforcing her parental authority had come at a price. "I still think I'd go for the french horn. You can always invest in earplugs."

"I'd rather invest in my daughter," Gray replied. Picking his car keys off a rack, he walked stiffly out of the room.

Ivy skipped breakfast and left for the ski hill with Gray and Halle. Norman was nowhere to be found, and by nine thirty the guests had also cleared out. This left Jamie with an empty house and a head full of thoughts she wasn't sure she wanted to have.

She wandered about the downstairs, cleaning up and pausing to examine pictures or knickknacks as if she were an archeologist trying to piece together an ancient civilization by the artifacts left behind. She found a wedding photo and several photographs of a dark-haired woman with wide-set eyes and a generous smile. Gray's wife—the ski champion.

She'd also been a mother, probably only a few years older than Jamie had been. She wondered if having a baby had been exciting for her or if she'd been as scared as Jamie.

She smiled, remembering the hours she'd spent rehearsing the kind of mother she'd be. In the afternoons, while Aunt Bea slept, she'd go into the kitchen and bake some type of sweet bread to tempt the old woman's appetite.

"This is how you knead dough," she explained to her unborn baby, all the while imagining a daughter or son working beside her, laughing at the sticky dough, and getting flour everywhere.

Of course, it hadn't happened the way she'd thought. She'd

been naive enough to imagine she would actually have time to bake with her child. Day care was a concept they hadn't taught in high school. Then again, even if they had, nothing could have prepared her for the physical wrench that had torn through her the first day—and every day after that—when she'd left Ivy at Small Blessings.

After she checked in with her office—no messages, no new listings, no surprise there—Jamie headed for the ski hill. She rode to the top of the mountain in the double chairlift next to a middle-aged man in a bulky blue snowsuit.

"So how's your day going?" Jamie gave him a friendly smile.

The man pulled the safety bar down, and the chair began to climb the hill. "Great. My kids are having a great time." He glanced sideways at her and looked quickly away, not returning the smile she gave him. "My wife is enjoying a day without kids. She homeschools them—all four of them."

"Oh," Jamie said. "That's got to be a lot of hard work."

The man seemed more than happy to discuss in detail just how much work homeschooling entailed. He seemed to insert "my wife" or "my wife and I" into every sentence and addressed the air straight in front of him. Jamie, at first, was amused. The guy must have mistaken her politeness for something more. But then it occurred to her that he might be picking up a vibe from her—some fragment of availability or, heaven forbid, particles of loneliness that clung to her like a dusting of snow.

She couldn't wait to dismount from the lift, and purposely headed in the opposite direction when they skied off. She followed a group of snowboarders who were headed for the Queen of Hearts. It was a good distance from the lift, and the snowboarders were soon out of sight. Jamie gamely continued poling across the top of the mountain. Soon Jamie started to sweat. She paused to catch her breath.

There wasn't another skier in sight, and the only noise was the huffing of her breath. Surrounded by pines and snow, Jamie thought the world looked pristine and perfect. She exhaled frosty plumes and watched them disappear. It was so still here. So peaceful. So *unspoiled*. She leaned her weight on her ski poles and felt the rapid *thump-thump-thump* of her heart.

*I've been living above my means*, she admitted. *I'm alienated from my family, and now even my daughter isn't talking to me.* She closed her eyes. *I can't do this anymore. I am so tired of worrying about things and trying to do everything by myself.*

She lifted her face to the vast gray sky. *I don't know what to do.*

A deep, cold wind sliced across the mountaintop. She heard the trees groan, then the world became still once more.

Something stirred deep in Jamie's heart. She looked around the woods. *Just who*, she thought, *am I talking to?*

# twelve

Jamie was standing on a chair helping Norman string lights around the windows in the lodge when Gray came in from teaching. Norman handed Gray the staple gun. "Help me out, Gray. Staple the cord while I go to the storage room and get the garlands."

He scurried off, leaving Jamie alone with Gray and the uncomfortable echoes of the discussion they'd had earlier that morning. She stretched the light cord higher on the wall and reached with her free hand for the staple gun.

"Let me do it," Gray said.

"I'm fine," Jamie said.

"I know," Gray said. "But I can reach more easily."

Jamie could feel the blood running out of her arm and her fingers turning weak from lack of circulation. "That might be true, but my line will be straighter than yours."

"How do you know?"

"Because I see your old staple holes. They're all over the place." She could fix them with a little putty and a can of paint.

"How do you know they're my holes?" Gray argued.

"Because Norman told me," Jamie said, smiling, although he couldn't see it. "He also told me about the time you stapled his sleeve to the wall."

"He moved his arm at the last minute."

"Which he said was a good thing."

She and Gray laughed, and it seemed to ease some of the tension between them. He was right about one thing, though. She needed his help to reach the top of the window. Reluctantly, she stepped off the chair and passed the staple gun to

Gray. "Be careful," she warned. "I don't want to have to explain anything to Norman."

He got to work. She studied the powerful set of his shoulders and the sunlight glinting in his thick brown hair. The cut was a little shaggy, and his brown ski sweater had a small tear on the side seam. He'd never be the kind of guy who'd be comfortable with a sleek, short haircut or a button-down shirt of Egyptian cotton, but there was a solidness about him that Jamie found extremely appealing. Not that she was going to let herself get involved. Jamie King stood on her own two feet. Maybe she wasn't the Lone Ranger, but she wasn't dependent upon anyone, either.

"Look," she said matter-of-factly. "About this morning, I'm sorry." She swallowed and pushed forward. "I'm the last person who should be giving you parental advice. You should give Halle the skis if you think that's best." She untangled another length of cord as Gray reached higher around the window.

He stapled another length into place. "Don't worry about it."

She could leave it at that, but something in her needed to explain. "I wouldn't have opened my mouth, but I started remembering what it was like when I was Halle's age." She focused her gaze out the window at the white mountain filling almost all the space her eye could see. "My parents had some pretty big expectations for me. I never felt like I could live up to them."

"I'm sure your parents only set high standards because they saw something good in you."

Jamie's lips twisted. If he only knew the irony of that statement. "Maybe," she agreed. "But it was hard, Gray. Always pushing myself, trying to be what they wanted. I wasn't nearly as academic as they would have liked, and if it hadn't been for a lot of private tumbling lessons and a very strict diet, I never would have made varsity cheerleader."

"Why didn't you just tell your parents you felt they were pushing you too hard?"

Jamie shrugged. "It was complicated. But the more I achieved, it seemed the higher I flew and the farther I'd have to fall."

He climbed off the chair and looked at her for a very long time. "I'm sorry that happened to you," he said. "But it's a different story with Halle."

"I know," Jamie said. "I've seen the two of you together. You've got a great relationship." She glanced over as Norman returned with a box overflowing with garlands. "Hey, Gray, here comes your dad." She felt exposed, as if she'd said too much about herself and was eager to lighten the moment. "Give me your arm. Let's pretend I stapled your sleeve to the wall."

&

The next several days passed in a blur of activity. Before she knew it, it was Christmas Eve, and Jamie was helping Norman arrange the picnic tables in the après ski room. Although Jamie was looking forward to the Torchlight Parade, she was dreading Christmas Day. Always in the past she'd managed to give Ivy really great presents—a shopping trip to Manhattan or a makeover for Ivy's bedroom. One year she'd even leased her a Thoroughbred horse.

This year would be very different.

"A little more to the right," Norman instructed. "We still need to fit about two more tables under the windows for the buffet."

The picnic table scraped the floor as Jamie shoved it into place. Straightening, she rubbed the small of her back. Gray had wanted to help them, but the J-bar had broken down and he'd had to fix it. "Hold on, Norman," she said as he singlehandedly tried to move another table. As she moved to help him, a burly guy in ski bibs and a red thermal shirt stepped in to help.

Jamie took Norman's arm and pulled him away. "Why don't you sit down for a moment?"

"Don't fuss," Norman said, but allowed her to lead him to a picnic bench.

"I'm not fussing," Jamie said. "I'm taking a break. With you."

"When I was in the army," Norman stated, mopping his brow with a handkerchief, "we did a lot tougher things. Like drive tanks."

"You get to sit down when you drive a tank," Jamie pointed out. "You want something to drink?"

Norman mopped his face and then stuck the crumbled handkerchief into the pocket of his jeans. "What time is it, Jamie?"

"Getting close to five o'clock."

Norman groaned. "People are coming in two hours. We still have to put out the tablecloths, hot water, cocoa packets, cups, napkins, doughnuts. I have to set up Santa's chair—it always goes right next to the Christmas tree in the corner—and Santa's bag is back at the house and isn't even ready. The torches haven't been checked. How did we get so late this year?"

Jamie studied the deep lines etched across Norman's freckled face. His brown eyes were full of worry. "Let me drive you back to the house," she offered. "You can get Santa's bag ready, and I'll take care of the rest."

He shook his head. "There's too much that still needs to be done."

"Don't worry," Jamie said, smiling. "I'll get it done. I know a lot about running open houses, remember?"

An hour and a half later, Jamie put her hands on her hips and admired the room. The picnic tables looked cheerful with their bright red tablecloths and centerpieces of fresh pine boughs and silver balls. She'd moved around some of the ornaments on the Christmas tree so people could see them better. Turning on the tree lights, she admired the shimmering pine, which was as perfect as she could make it.

All she needed was a chair for Santa. She dragged Gray's rolling office chair into place beside the tree and threw a red blanket with white fur trim over the seat. Giving one last look at the fire blazing in the stone fireplace and the lights blinking on the Christmas tree, she hurried to the lady's changing room to put on her ski clothes.

Norman hadn't returned from the house, and she didn't see him as she joined the crowd gathering just outside the lodge. She saw Gray passing out flashlights. He had a fur-trimmed Santa's hat anchored on his head with his ski goggles.

"Nice hat, Gray," she called.

"Thanks. Where's yours?" He grinned across the space between them.

Jamie touched her white headband. "Right here."

"I don't think Santa's helpers wear headbands," Gray admonished her.

"I don't think they wear ski parkas or goggles, either," Jamie replied.

He laughed and then waved with his hands to get the crowd's attention. Cupping his hands together, he shouted over the roar of voices. "Time to head for the lifts."

A cheer went up, and a massive traffic jam formed as everyone skied over to the double chairlift. Jamie glimpsed Halle getting onto the lift with Gray and the two of them swinging up into the dark, frosty night. She glimpsed Ivy standing in line with Ella. Obviously Ivy didn't want to ride the lift with Jamie.

She ended up seated with a man who kept leaning over the back of the chair to talk to his wife and daughter who were riding in the chair behind theirs. She didn't try to engage him. Instead she thought about the upcoming service at the top of the mountain. She hadn't been to church in fourteen years. Hadn't thought she belonged. Her thoughts drifted far past the dark borders of the pines.

"Are you gaining weight, honey?" Jamie's mother commented as Jamie walked over to the glossy black Lincoln Continental. It was Sunday morning, and they were getting ready to go to church. "Bill? You think she should change into a different dress?"

Jamie ducked into the backseat before the critical gaze of

her father turned to her. She'd been hiding the weight gain and the morning sickness for weeks now, praying for her parents to notice something was wrong and terrified at what would happen when they did.

"We're late," Jamie's father replied, getting into the driver's seat. "She's fine."

"You didn't look," Jamie's mother complained. "She's about to pop out of that dress."

Jamie wrapped her thin cardigan more tightly around herself. The July morning was hot, but the sweater was one of the few items she owned that didn't strain against the new curves of her body. She looked out the car window and wondered how much longer she could disguise herself. Her mother wanted to take her clothes shopping, and her friends wanted to know why she wouldn't go to the pool with them. She was so tired of making up excuses, of the fear inside that seemed to grow as steadily as the baby inside her.

"You need to put yourself on a diet," Jamie's mother said firmly. "You don't want people looking at you and wondering why such a pretty girl would let herself go like that."

Jamie shut her eyes and tried to squeeze back the tears that came so easily now. She'd been praying for answers but felt more alone than she'd ever been in her life. Devon, since that awful night in the YMCA parking lot, hadn't returned any of her calls. She hadn't told a single one of her friends, either, and the burden of her secret felt increasingly like a weight she couldn't carry. Her mother was going on and on about the evils of carbohydrates and the importance of disciplined eating habits as they turned into the church's driveway.

As they passed three huge wooden crosses, Jamie looked at the center one and thought about Jesus, about how brave He'd been to be crucified for the sins of the world. She should be brave, too. Before she lost her nerve, she blurted out, "I'm not getting fat. I'm pregnant."

There was a moment of silence, then Jamie's mother turned

around and looked at her. The gaze seemed to burn straight through the white cardigan and sundress. "Bill, turn the car around. Church is the last place we need to be right now." She smiled, but it scared Jamie more than reassured her. "Who else knows, Jamie?"

Jamie mumbled Devon's name. It wasn't as if they wouldn't guess. After all, he'd been her only boyfriend. She tried to read her mother's face in the silence that followed. She expected disappointment, shock, even anger. Her mother's calmness caught her off guard, and she felt hopeful that it wasn't going to be as bad as she'd feared.

Jamie gripped the cold safety bar more tightly as the lift chair traveled through the night. It hadn't been as bad as she'd feared. The weeks following her disclosure had been far worse.

The mountain felt about ten degrees colder at the top. Jamie tucked her chin into the warmth of her jacket and followed the crowd to the top of Alice's Alley. Over the top of heads she glimpsed Ivy, who was standing by herself at the edge of the trail. Pushing through the throng of people, Jamie shuffled over to her. "Hey," she said. "Look at the stars."

"Yeah," Ivy agreed. "This is so cool, Mom."

Jamie savored the fragile connection between them. "The night you were born was like this. Aunt Bea looked out the window and said every star was shining."

"She was weak from the chemotherapy," Ivy said, picking up the story. "But that night she was strong."

"Strong enough to drive me to the hospital and strong enough to hold my hand while you were being born. She was the first one to hold you, Ivy, besides the nurse and doctor. She loved you. I wish she could have known you."

"May I have your attention please," Gray's voice boomed through a megaphone. "In a few minutes, Reverend Thomas Blaymires is going to say a few words, then we're going to ski single file down the mountain." He gave them some safety pointers and promised to be at the end of the line if anyone needed help. He passed the megaphone to the reverend.

"Good evening," Reverend Blaymires began. "I'm honored to be with you on this Christmas Eve." He had a Bible in his hands. "From the book of Luke." He paused. " 'And there were shepherds living out in the fields nearby, keeping watch over their flocks at night. An angel of the Lord appeared to them. . . .' "

The stars seemed to hang right over her head, and the night air was as pure and cold as chilled water. Tears swelled in Jamie's eyes and turned to icy streaks on her cold cheeks. She wiped them away quickly before Ivy could see and ask why Jamie was crying. She bit her lip hard and willed away the grief that rose and swirled and clogged her throat. She was suddenly so cold and so raw inside, as if the reverend's words were a wind that sliced through her, reminding her painfully that she had been raised in a family that went to church, that heard the words from Luke every Christmas Eve, but that family was lost to her. Even the comfort she might have gotten from God was lost to her. One by circumstance, the other by choice.

She looked at Ivy. Her beautiful, shining girl. Even in the poor lighting cast by the trail lights hanging in the trees, Jamie could see the radiance in her daughter's face as she listened to the reverend's words. *How can I look at her and have regrets? Everything that's happened to me is worth it,* Jamie assured herself.

*Everything?* a small voice inside asked.

*Everything,* Jamie agreed firmly.

❧

The reverend ended his reading. "Merry Christmas," he said. "May the love of God shine through you onto others. Amen." He turned on his flashlight, and everyone else did the same. The sudden light was blinding after standing in the darkness.

The first skier began to descend the mountain, followed by another, then another. Soon a string of lights was snaking its way down the hill. Flanked by the trail lights, their flashlights burned as bright as fire in the darkness.

Finally, it was Ivy's turn, then Jamie's. She clutched the flashlight in her left hand and held it up like a torch. It felt a little awkward to ski without her poles, but it also made her feel lighter and freer and strangely exhilarated, as if very little gravity held her onto the mountain, and if she wanted to, she could fly through the darkness and into the stars shining so brightly over the valley below.

The party was already under way by the time Jamie put away her skis and joined the others in the après ski room. There had to be at least two hundred people laughing and talking. Someone had brought out a karaoke machine, and above the roar of voices, a gray-haired woman with a very shaky soprano was belting out an enthusiastic "O Come All Ye Faithful."

Jamie poured herself a cup of hot chocolate and added a generous helping of marshmallows. She was thinking about going for a doughnut when a deep voice said, "You look very familiar to me. Have we met?"

She turned. A large, heavyset man with silver hair and ruddy cheeks was looking down at her. "Gus Peters?" She felt the skin on the back of her neck prickle with excitement. She held out her hand. "I'm Jamie King. We met last year at the Connecticut Home Seekers banquet last spring. I loved your keynote address."

His eyes lit up with recollection. "Of course. I never forget a beautiful face. Now tell me. What are you doing here? Business or pleasure?"

"A little of both. I'm vacationing with my daughter—she's on break from Miss Porter's." She sipped her hot chocolate as her mind whirled. "How about you?"

"I'm visiting the grandkids. They love the Torchlight Parade." His cell phone rang. "Excuse me, but I've got to take this call." He slipped off into the crowd.

Jamie watched his back until it disappeared. She had a top-notch land developer and Gray in the same room. If she could get them together, there was a chance she could turn the conversation to the topic of real estate. More specifically, the future of Pilgrim's Peak. Something inside told her Christmas Eve was not the right time to discuss this, but she decided to hunt down Gray.

She found him deep in conversation with a small group. Before she could get his attention, however, a gravelly voice called out, "Ho! Ho! Ho!" and Santa walked into the room. A golden retriever, wearing antlers and carrying a red tennis ball in its mouth, walked at his side. At least a dozen kids rushed forward crying, "Santa! Santa!"

"Ho! Ho! Ho!" Norman boomed, bending to hug the kids who nearly knocked him over as they swarmed him.

"Let Santa get to his chair," Gray said. "Then I think there's a small present for each of you." He lifted the red velvet bag from Norman's shoulder.

Norman—who had at least three pillows stuffed beneath his Santa suit—clumped over to the chair by the tree. When he sat, there was a great whooshing noise and a few down feathers flew out from beneath his coat. "Santa's molting," he said in a stage whisper.

Boomer ducked out of his antlers and trotted off to Halle, who was standing in line for a turn at the karaoke machine. A couple of the smaller kids ran after Boomer. Boomer dropped his ball and began happily licking the small faces around him.

"Oh no," Gray muttered and then called out, "Don't throw. . ."

The ball sailed out of the little boy's hands. Boomer took off like a shot, cutting a swath through the crowded room. People cried out as the dog ran between their legs, or knocked into their knees, or narrowly avoided bowling them over. The golden almost reached the tennis ball, but then someone kicked it. The ball rolled under the tree, and Boomer dove in after it. Jamie heard the ornaments jingle.

"Get away from the tree," Gray yelled, motioning with his arm.

Boomer emerged from beneath the limbs, tail wagging and tennis ball firmly in his jaws. He trotted safely away as the tree began to topple.

"Timber!" Norman shouted, moving away faster than Jamie had ever seen him move.

The tree fell to the side, landing squarely on the picnic table, squashing several boxes of doughnuts and toppling a plastic punch bowl. A river of ginger ale and grape juice gushed across the floor, carrying with it a variety of sprinkled, cream, and glazed doughnuts.

Everyone seemed to freeze in place. Even the karaoke singer paused as everyone stared at the Christmas tree on top of the refreshments table. Jamie looked at Gray. She thought about how upset her parents would have been if something like this had happened at one of their parties. Gray, however, began to laugh.

"You know what they say," Norman announced cheerfully. "It's not a Christmas party until the tree falls over."

Somebody started to applaud, and then everybody was talking at once, straightening the fallen tree and cleaning up the spilled punch. Jamie had just finished mopping the floor when Gray walked over to her. "You need any help?"

"Nope, almost finished." She straightened and pushed her bangs behind her ear. Out of the corner of her eye, she spotted Boomer. The dog had his head in a plastic garbage bag, which was slumped on the floor. She watched Boomer's head emerge with a squashed doughnut in his jaws. "Boomer digests doughnuts, right?"

Jamie met Gray's gaze, and they both laughed. "Can we open a window?" she asked. "I think Boomer is preparing to boom."

# thirteen

It was snowing lightly on Christmas morning. Jamie let Boomer outside. The sun hadn't risen yet, but the porch lights illuminated a white veil of snow against a black velvet background. She hugged herself and smiled. A white Christmas in an old Victorian house surrounded by mountains and woods. It might not be Aspen, but it was lovely. No matter what Ivy said, some small part of her had to be glad she was here with Jamie.

She made coffee and was just putting a pan of sticky buns—Ivy's favorite—in the oven when Gray, Norman, and Halle walked into the kitchen. Halle was still in her pajamas and wearing a fluffy pink bathrobe. With her rumpled, thick hair and huge brown eyes, she looked more like a little kid than a teenager. "Merry Christmas, Halle," Jamie said and gave the girl a hug.

"One for me," Norman quipped. When Jamie gave him a squeeze, he kissed her cheek. "Merry Christmas, sweetheart," he said.

It seemed awkward to ignore Gray, so she hugged him lightly, too. "Merry Christmas, Gray."

His flannel shirt felt incredibly soft against her cheek in contrast to his chest, which was rock hard. Although she wanted to be impervious to the clean man scent that clung to him, she wasn't. When she let go of him, she hurried to the oven and pretended to be absorbed in adjusting the temperature.

"Can I open my stocking now?" Halle asked.

"Sure," Gray replied. He started to head for the family room, but stopped. "Come with us, Jamie."

She waved them off. "Oh, you guys go on. I've got a little more to do here."

"It's Christmas," Norman stated kindly. "We don't want you working all day in the kitchen."

"I know, but I still have some work to do on the buffet." Jamie wiped her hands on her apron. Probably the Westlers would rather open their gifts in private. Besides, Ivy was still sleeping, and it wouldn't be right to start Christmas without her.

"The buffet is perfect," Gray said.

"But the sticky buns. . ."

"Still need time to cook. Come on," Gray urged.

Jamie laughed as Gray took one of her hands and Halle the other and literally pulled her toward the family room. The tree with its funny branchlike nose was lit, and there were two stockings hanging from the mantel—one for Halle and the other for Boomer. Jamie's gaze settled on the Nativity scene on the top of the wooden mantel. Last night the manger had been empty, but this morning there was a tiny baby inside the straw.

"You okay?" Gray asked.

She smiled automatically, but something must have showed on her face because Norman patted her arm gently. "I know just how you feel. Every Christmas morning I feel like the luckiest man on the earth."

"Here's your bone, Boomer," Halle extracted a large knucklebone from the dog's stocking. Boomer politely wagged his tail and took it from the girl's hands.

As Jamie watched Halle lift her stocking, she realized she wanted Ivy to be there, too. She didn't have a lot of presents for her daughter, but she had filled a stocking with Ivy's favorite candy—Sour Patch Kids—and inexpensive beauty products she'd bought at the grocery store. She excused herself and hurried up the steps. "Ivy." She gently shook the girl's shoulder, which felt as thin as a fin under the blanket. "Wake up, honey. Merry Christmas."

Ivy turned and blinked sleepily at her. "What time is it?"

"Almost seven."

Ivy groaned and tried to pull the covers over her head.

"Halle, Norman, and Gray are starting to open presents. I thought you might like to be part of it."

The lump under the covers made another unintelligible sound.

"Come on, honey. You don't want to miss anything." She tugged at the covers, and when Ivy resisted her attempts, she increased her efforts until it was a tug-of-war match. Then, with a final wrench, Jamie pulled them free. Ivy lay on her back, glaring at her.

"It's snowing," Jamie said brightly to cover her dismay at Ivy's expression. "You should see how pretty it looks!"

"I'd rather sleep," Ivy said and snatched the blanket over her head.

Jamie's stomach tightened with the knowledge that Ivy wasn't excited about Christmas—or was it just that she wasn't excited about spending it with Jamie? Or was Ivy just a typical teenager who wanted to sleep? Jamie wasn't sure of anything anymore.

"I made sticky buns—your favorite. But I can't guarantee there'll be any left if you wait much longer." She moved to the door. "They're warm and gooey, with raisins and cinnamon and cream cheese frosting. . . ."

The figure groaned, but the covers moved. Jamie decided to take this as a good sign.

❧

Gray blinked as his dad fired off a shot with the camera. His father never asked anyone to pose and had an uncanny ability to sneak up and take the most unflattering picture of a person's life. His father never seemed to mind that he chopped off people's heads or caught them with their mouths hanging open.

"Grandpa!" Halle complained as his father pointed the camera at her. "I haven't done my hair yet."

"You don't need to. It's supposed to be a candid."

Gray looked up as Jamie came into the room. She had a tight look about the mouth, which his father immediately immortalized with the camera. She'd probably want to burn that picture. Gray gave her a sympathetic smile. "Is Ivy coming down?"

"I think so, but don't wait. It could be awhile."

Halle dove into her stocking. It contained the same things it did every year—a bottle of vitamins, wool socks, a giant chocolate bar, a stuffed animal, a book of Life Savers, and an orange at the toe. This year Gray had added a sterling silver ring that had belonged to Lonna. He watched Halle's eyes grow wide as she pulled it out of the box and held it to the light.

"It was your mother's," he said, although he was pretty sure she realized this. "I thought your finger might be big enough to wear it now."

She slipped it on the fourth finger of her right hand and held it up for him to admire. "Looks good," Gray said.

Halle held her hand out to Jamie. "It's beautiful, honey," Jamie said. "There's something small under the tree from me that might go with that."

Halle spotted Jamie's box immediately. She ripped the wrapping paper off and held up a sterling silver bracelet. "Oh my gosh," she cried. "It's beautiful. Thank you, Miss Jamie."

Gray almost corrected Halle, but stopped himself. He hadn't thought of Jamie as "Miss King" in days. If Halle wanted to call her "Miss Jamie," he didn't see the harm of it.

"You're welcome, honey." Jamie stood to hug her. Just as she put her arms around Halle, Ivy walked into the room.

"Merry Christmas, Ivy," Gray said, rising with the thought of giving her a hug, but then stopped at the look of hurt on Ivy's face. "We're just getting started."

"Merry Christmas, honey," Jamie stepped away from Halle. Her hands fluttered. "You want something to drink?"

"Coffee," Ivy said. "Black."

Jamie's lips twisted. "How about hot chocolate?"

"My friends and I walk to a coffee shop in Farmington all the time."

"I'll make her a cup." Gray winked at Jamie, hoping she would trust him. "It's a flavored coffee—decaf. You'll like it, Ivy."

When he came back into the room, Ivy was holding a jewelry box in her hand and wearing an unhappy expression. "What'd you get, Ivy?"

"Earrings," she said. "Just like my mom's."

He peeked into the velvet box. A pair of diamond studs winked back at him, and true enough, they looked exactly like the ones sitting in the lobes of Jamie's ears. "They're lovely," he said.

"Thanks."

Gray gave Jamie a sympathetic smile. He remembered the year he'd given Halle the wrong American Girl doll. Polly? Molly? He'd felt like the worst parent in the world. But how could Ivy be disappointed with such a beautiful gift? He pondered the question as he reached beneath the tree. "Here's one with your name on it, Dad." He tossed his father a box.

"It's from me, Grandpa," Halle said.

His dad ripped off the paper. "A Chia Head!" He sounded as if nothing could have pleased him more, then he looked at Halle. "What's a Chia Head?"

"You water the head, and grass grows like hair, Grandpa," Halle explained. "Then you cut it with scissors to style it."

"I'll be a monkey's uncle," Norman said, turning the box slowly in his hands. "Too bad someone can't figure out the same thing for growing hair on people."

"They have, Dad," Gray said. "It's called Rogaine."

His father grinned. "And how would you know about Rogaine? Personal experience?" He winked at Jamie.

Gray ran his hand through his hair. "Nope. From the TV, Dad. Some of us actually stay awake for an entire program."

"Some of us don't care for the programs. There's either too much violence or people mumble and you can't understand them." He gestured to Halle. "There's something for you and something for Ivy under the tree."

Halle dove beneath the tree and found the gifts in about five seconds. The two girls sat next to each other on the rug and simultaneously ripped off the wrapping paper. "Oh Grandpa, it's beautiful," Halle cried out, holding up a brand-new sweater. "It's from my favorite store and is just the right size!"

"Good job, Dad."

His father nodded and winked at Jamie, leaving Gray no doubt as to who had picked out the sweater.

"Mr. Westler," Ivy said rather shyly, holding up leather ski gloves. "Thank you so much. I love them."

"They're racing gloves," his dad said proudly. "Thought they might come in handy for you."

After a brief break for breakfast, more presents were exchanged. Gray opened an electric razor from his father—and took some ribbing about needing to use it—a book from Halle written by a Christian author he particularly liked, and thick wool socks from Boomer.

Jamie opened up a box of chocolates from his father. She also received a framed photo of Ivy smiling next to a big white sign that said MISS PORTER'S SCHOOL, FOUNDED 1843. Gray found himself wishing he'd bought Jamie a gift, especially when she handed him a tin of homemade chocolate peanut butter fudge.

"There's something else for you, Halle, behind the tree," Gray prompted after almost all the other gifts had been opened.

Halle dragged out the long, tall box he'd tucked behind the branches. He knew, though, from her expression that she'd seen it all along and had been waiting to open it. He found himself holding his breath as she examined the size and weight of the box.

"What do you think it is?" Gray was unable to resist asking.

"Skis?" Halle guessed.

"Open it," he pressed gently.

She did. Her nose wrinkled in confusion as she tore off the

green and red paper and saw the brand name of a company that made ski racks for cars. "A ski rack, Dad?"

"What every girl needs," Gray said, trying not to smile.

Halle began to pull out the wads of tissue paper, then she found the leather case. "Is this. . .?" Her face turned rapturous. "Oh Dad. . .did you. . .?"

"I don't know," Gray said innocently, enjoying the light that had come into his daughter's eyes.

Halle's fingers clicked open the bindings as she pulled out the shiny brass horn. She looked over at him, rapturous. "You're kidding me. You got this? You went on eBay?"

"Go on," Gray urged. "You can actually hold it."

She took her time pulling it from the case, then held it reverently against her chest. "It's so beautiful," she said. "Thank you so, so much, Dad."

She studied every gleaming inch before bringing it to her mouth. Closing her eyes she took a deep breath and put her lips against the mouthpiece. Gray heard air passing through the instrument. Halle took another deep breath and tried again. This time she managed to produce a low, wheezy-sounding note that unexpectedly jumped several octaves. When she ran out of breath, she put the instrument down and looked at him triumphantly.

"That was great, honey," Gray said, struggling to sound sincere.

"Want to hear it again?" She already had the instrument to her lips and was summoning forth the breath needed to produce that awful sound again. He looked over at Jamie, who was smiling from ear to ear. His dad, however, was doing the only thing that made sense, and that was leaving the room.

"Where you going, Dad?" Gray asked.

His father glanced over his shoulder and grinned. "I'm going to get my bugle, sonny boy, so Halle and I can jam together."

# fourteen

After lunch Gray, Halle, Ivy, and Jamie went for a walk. Norman stayed home to watch the Sugar Bowl on television. The snow was deeper than her boots, and Jamie felt like some sort of wilderness survivor as she stepped onto the road, which was no longer a road at all, but part of the scenic white landscape. "It's beautiful," she breathed. "Simply beautiful."

"And quiet," Grayson agreed, appearing by her side. "Blessedly quiet."

Jamie watched their two daughters, who had run a short distance ahead, plow through the unbroken path. They were purposely leaving long lines in the pristine blanket of snow. "You did the right thing, Grayson, giving her that french horn. Did you see her face?"

"Yeah," he said. "And did you hear the noise she made? It's lucky we don't live in Africa. Every mother elephant within hearing range would have come running."

Jamie laughed. "She'll get better."

"I thought a lot about what you told me," Gray admitted. "I don't ever want her to feel pressure to ski." He gave her a sideways glance. "However, her birthday is coming up in February, so I might give her an early present."

"French horn lessons, right?"

He laughed and bumped her shoulder playfully. "She'll get those, but she'll also be getting new skis."

Jamie laughed and bumped him back. "But no pressure to race, right?"

"When she skis on them," Gray stated with confidence, "she'll want to race."

Jamie didn't want to spoil Gray's daydream, but she wondered if he realized how much Halle was drawn to a world

93

that had little to do with skiing. On more than one occasion the girl had pumped Jamie for tips on hair and makeup, and Halle's eyes lit up when she talked about band, especially the marching band, which she'd seen perform last fall.

They hiked to the ski lodge, which no longer looked slightly dilapidated. Under its thick coat of fresh snow, it seemed rustic and charming. Sturdy and inviting, it sat like a refuge beneath the huge, snowy mountain looming behind it.

"Dad!" Halle called and then flopped onto the snowy ground. "Look." She spread her arms and legs and made a snow angel. To Jamie's amazement, Ivy did the same thing. Before she thought too much about it, she flopped down and made a snow angel, too. Gray did the same, and soon the four of them were admiring the four imprints on the ground.

They wandered to the back of the lodge. It seemed strange to see the lift still, the cable carrying a line of snow up the mountain.

"Let's build a snowman," Halle suggested, already crouching to pack as much snow as she could into a ball. Ivy bent to help her.

Jamie snapped a photo with her cell phone of the two girls working together. Kneeling, she began to build her own snowman. Next to her, Gray did the same. His snowball was larger, but significantly lopsided.

"I see we're going for a snowman with personality."

Gray looked up. He had snowflakes on his dark eyelashes, and his nose was red from the cold. "And you're going for a miniature one."

"It will be smaller," Jamie agreed. "But perfectly shaped."

"Until someone steps on it," Gray teased.

"I would rather have someone step on my snowman than have it look like a Mr. Potato Head."

"Not everything has to look perfect, Mom," Ivy announced. "I like the way Mr. Westler's snowman looks."

The unexpected harshness of Ivy's words hurt. Jamie ducked

her head before anyone saw, and she barely heard Gray tell Ivy to call him Mr. Grayson. Ivy didn't mean to sound so harsh, she tried to assure herself. Ivy was just at that age where everything Jamie did or said was wrong. She packed some snow onto the ball and hoped someday Ivy would appreciate and understand the choices Jamie had had to make.

Gray rolled his lopsided ball over to hers. "If we pool our talents," he suggested, "we could build a really nice snowman."

Jamie glanced up at him through the falling snow. She didn't want his pity, but it seemed churlish to refuse his offer. "Sure," she said. "Do you want to make a girl snowman or a boy snowman?"

Grayson cocked his head. "We're not shaping an anatomically correct snowman, are we?"

"Of course not," Jamie stated. "I just thought it would be nice to build a snow couple."

"We'll make the girl snowman," Halle cried. "I have an old pink scarf and some rhinestone buttons from my Halloween costume. We'll give her earrings, too."

"Want my diamond studs?" Ivy offered. Just as Jamie was about to lay down the law about that, Ivy turned to her, grinning. "I'm just kidding, Mom."

Jamie exhaled slowly. "You had me for a moment there."

"I know," Ivy said. "I couldn't resist it."

Her daughter gave her an impish grin—one Jamie recognized from years past—and then went back to work on the snow girl. Jamie stared at her daughter's back, appreciating for maybe the first time how her mother used to look at her sometimes, as if Jamie had arrived on earth straight from Mars.

About an hour later, Jamie stepped back to admire their snow boy. "He looks exactly like their snow girl," she commented to Gray, who was beginning to look a little bit like a snowman himself with all the falling snow that had collected on his shoulders.

"That's only because their snow girl is pretty muscular.

Tomorrow we'll put a cowboy hat on ours, and he'll look a lot more macho." He turned to the girls who were huddled a short distance away and appeared to be whispering to each other. "Hey, girls, how about some hot chocolate?"

Instead of replying, Halle launched a snowball at him. Ivy threw one at Jamie, who quickly ducked behind the snow boy. Gray dropped to the ground and began forming snowballs as the girls pelted his stationary form.

"Gray," Jamie shouted. "Retreat!"

"Never!" He dodged one snowball and laughed as another exploded across his chest. "Okay," he said. "You asked for it." He launched a snowball at Halle, hitting her leg. He aimed a second ball at Ivy, who launched a ball at him at the same time. The two snowballs collided in midair.

Jamie scurried out, clutching two snowballs. She handed one to Gray and threw the other at Halle, missing by a mile. As Jamie rearmed, Ivy moved in and began pelting her with a seemingly endless supply of snowballs. Jamie's hat joined Gray's on the snowy ground. "Hey! That's cashmere!" Jamie said.

Ivy grinned. "I know."

"Okay. It's war now." Jamie straightened, clutching a snowball. Ivy also had one final ball in her hands. "Okay, then. On the count of three," Jamie said soberly. "One, two, three. . ." She closed her eyes and threw her snowball well to the side of her daughter. At the same time, an icy fist exploded across her face. She jerked back, wiping the clumps of snow from her eyes and cheeks.

"Game over," Gray announced. He positioned himself at Jamie's side. "You okay?"

Jamie's face burned from the cold. "I'm fine. No big deal."

"You can take a free shot at me," Ivy offered. "And I'll even stand close enough so you won't miss."

Jamie shook her head. "Don't worry about it, Ivy. I just need to check my contact lens."

"We can go inside the lodge," Gray suggested.

"You sure you're okay, Mom? Seriously. I thought you'd duck. Why didn't you?"

*Because I never thought you'd aim for my head.* "I don't know," Jamie said. "Been a long time since I was in a snowball fight."

Ivy hesitated, as if she might say something else, then ran to catch up with Halle.

Gray fell into step as they headed for the lodge. "You missed Ivy by a good six feet. You weren't even aiming for her, were you?" He was walking so close she could hear the whisper of his ski clothing chafing.

"Nope," Jamie admitted. "But don't tell her that. She'd only feel worse." But would she? Although she didn't want to admit it, Jamie knew the snowball to her head hadn't been an accident. Devon had been a terrific athlete, and so was Ivy. She stopped just in front of the lodge. "How do you do it? The whole single-parent thing?"

Gray laughed. "You just haven't seen our less than perfect moments."

"Well, she's turning out great."

"So is Ivy."

Jamie glanced sideways at his face. "Are you serious?" Her face tingled from the cold, and she could feel snow melting uncomfortably down her neck.

"She hangs on every word my dad says, and the other day I saw her helping a novice skier who was having some trouble on White Rabbit."

Jamie thought about this. "Then why is she so awful to me? Everything is a battle. I don't see why she doesn't realize I'm trying to look out for her, not make her life miserable." She clenched her hands into fists. "What's your secret?"

"No secret," Grayson said. He opened the heavy wooden door to the lodge and stepped back to let her pass. "I pray for her constantly. Every single night I'm on my knees by the side of my bed."

"And God tells you what to do?" Jamie honestly wanted to know.

"Not in words, but I know He's listening and that helps."

Jamie paused in the door frame. "How do you know He's listening?"

"It's a feeling." The expression in Gray's eyes turned thoughtful. "It's like any relationship, I guess. The more time you spend with a person, the better you get to know him."

Jamie could feel the welcoming heat of the lodge contrasting with the coldness behind her. She needed help, but her situation was very different from Gray's. "What if a person did something wrong, but he or she is not entirely sorry for it, either. Would God want a relationship with that kind of person?"

"Absolutely," Grayson replied. "God loves everyone. He hates sin, but He loves the sinner—and basically that's all of us. There's nothing He can't forgive, and no situation He can't change for His glory." He looked into her eyes. "You should tell that person not to be afraid to talk to God."

But what would she say? *Hello, God, it's me, Jamie King. You know—the girl who messed up about thirteen years ago. Do You think we could just look past that and move forward?*

Jamie shook her head. She didn't think prayers worked like that. Besides, her parents had kicked her out, and there was no reason to think God would want her, either.

# fifteen

The day after Christmas was one of the busiest days of the year at Pilgrim's Peak. By noon his dad had run out of rental equipment, and the Looking Glass was beginning to remind Gray of rush hour on I-84. The ski patrol had its hands full, and the extra three college kids he'd hired during the break as instructors were booked solid with lessons. He'd known this day would be jam-packed, and yet he'd gone ahead and scheduled a private lesson with Jamie King.

He'd asked her casually after dinner last night. "Hey, Jamie. One more present." Then he'd handed her a Christmas card. Inside it he'd included a handmade coupon for a ski lesson with today's date and time written on it.

Now here he was, standing beside the chairlift, his heart beating in anticipation. Since when did he look forward so much to giving a lesson? Since never, maybe. She skied up to him, and his heart gave a small, excited leap. As they settled into the chairlift, he found himself sitting a little closer and studying her profile for clues that might explain just what it was about her that he found so compelling.

She felt his gaze, turned, and said, "What are you looking at?"

Caught, he tried to laugh it off. "You looked so serious just then. I was trying to figure out what you were thinking."

"Oh," she said. "Just something about Ivy."

"What about her?" Almost against his will, his gaze lowered to her lips, and he wondered what it would be like to kiss her. The thought seemed to release something pleasantly heavy inside that flowed through his veins.

"Well," Jamie said at last. "I've been thinking of what you said yesterday. About spending more time with someone in order to strengthen a relationship." Her brow furrowed. "Can you teach me to giant slalom in a week?"

"What?" The question was so far from his own chain of thoughts it took him a few seconds to process it.

"I want to enter the interclub race."

"Jamie, you're making good progress, but running gates is going to be tough for a beginner."

Her chin lifted. "I can do tough."

"Two weeks ago you were getting dragged up the bunny hill by the J-bar."

"And I would have made it to the top if you hadn't insisted that I let go."

He shifted on the bench seat. "It takes time to develop the skills you need for a ski race."

"I can do it," Jamie argued. "All you have to do is ski around the gates and not fall down."

He laughed at the gross oversimplification. "Jamie, you have to be able to hold an edge when you turn, control your speed, and stop at the end of the race. You wouldn't believe how many people I've fished out of the safety net."

"If you don't want to help me, just say so."

"I'm not saying that," Gray hedged. The chair jostled them slightly as it rolled across a support tower. "Why all of a sudden is this race so important to you?"

"Because I have to find a way to connect with her before she goes back to Miss Porter's." He heard an unaccustomed vulnerability creep into her voice. "I think I'm losing her."

He thought about it. If she'd given him any other reason, he'd never have agreed, but this one he understood. Where would he and Halle be without a shared love of skiing? Besides, if he didn't help her, she'd do it anyway. "You'll have to ski more," he said, "to build up your leg strength. And you'll need to follow my instructions to the letter."

The small hut at the top of the hill came into sight. They dismounted without incident, and he brought her to the top of

Alice's Alley. The first drop was the steepest, and he couldn't help a small glimmer of satisfaction at the way her lips thinned at the sight of the pitch.

"This is the hill we use for the race," he said. "Right now I only have three gates set, and they're a little farther down the hill. There will be twelve the day of the race, and they'll start at the top."

"I can do that," Jamie stated, but the way her gaze slid away from his, he knew she was a little afraid.

"We don't have to do this," he offered. "You can find another way to spend time with Ivy. You could take her to the Farmington mall or something."

Jamie shook her head. "It has to be this. It's the only way I'll earn her respect."

He held his breath as she pushed off the top of the hill. She skidded sideways on the first turn, but then recovered her balance. She'd improved considerably, but she still had a lot to learn. She struggled with the next turn, and he called out for her to unweight her uphill ski.

He insisted she rest just before they reached the area of the trail with the gates. Pulling up alongside her, Gray waited until her breathing slowed down.

"Okay," he said. "See those three gates down there? You want to ski as close as you can to them. You keep the green gates on your left side and the red ones on your right. I'll show you."

With a push of his ski poles, he headed down the hill. He kept his speed slow and exaggerated the up and down motion of the turns through the gates. Pausing at the side of the trail, he turned to watch her.

She picked up more speed than he would have liked, but managed to turn around the first gate. He held his breath as she headed toward the second gate, skied right past it, then gave a cute little wiggle turn and headed for the third gate, which she also gave a wide berth.

She skied toward him with her elbows out like wings. Her

legs were too straight and her hips too bent. She had no form at all, but she looked so adorable that he didn't have the heart to correct her.

"How was that, coach?"

"Not bad," he said.

Her grin grew bigger. "Can we try it again?"

He nodded, firmly ignoring the small voice that said he'd be late for his next lesson. "Yup," he said. "Try and come a little closer to the gates next time. You missed the second gate."

"I know," Jamie agreed. "I would have missed the third, too, but I hit a bump, and it slowed me down enough to turn."

She beamed up at him. He looked at those full, rosy lips and thought about kissing her. It seemed a little less crazy than before. With a sinking feeling he realized it wouldn't be long before the thought of kissing her was not crazy at all.

# sixteen

Jamie skied for several more hours before heading back to the house. Her lesson with Gray left her nearly light-headed with excitement. With a little more practice—and Gray's expert coaching—she was convinced she and Ivy would make a decent showing in the mother/daughter class in the ski race.

In the foyer, she checked the registration book. The Kilpatricks and Wongs had checked out, and the Banbridges, Gregorys, and Goldmans had checked in. A full house. She'd make her asparagus, tomato, and fontina cheese frittata for tomorrow morning. After a quick shower, she headed to the kitchen to help Norman with dinner.

When she stepped in the kitchen, she found him leaning heavily against the kitchen counter. "Norman," she said and hurried up to him. "Are you okay?"

"Oh sure," he replied, but he continued to lean on the counter and his face had a frightening grayish cast.

"Sit." Jamie helped him to a kitchen chair and studied him anxiously. "What happened?"

"I just got a little dizzy for a moment," Norman admitted. "I'm fine now."

"Your face barely has any color."

He waved away the hand she placed on his forehead. "Stop fussing. I'm fine."

"Maybe you ought to lie down," Jamie suggested. "I'll make dinner, and if you don't feel like coming downstairs, I'll bring a tray to your room."

Norman didn't seem to have the strength to argue. He leaned against her as she helped him to his room. She was surprised how thin and fragile he felt against her. She tucked him into

103

his bed and pulled an extra blanket over him. As she turned to leave, he caught her wrist. "Listen," he said, "let's not mention this to Gray. With the club race coming up, the last thing he needs is to have me on his mind."

Jamie frowned. "I think he should know, Norman."

"Know what? That I got a little dizzy?"

She hesitated. "You almost passed out, Norman. Maybe you should see a doctor."

"They'll keep me waiting for hours in a room full of sick people," Norman stated firmly. "All I need is a little rest. Don't treat me like a child. I'm seventy-seven years old and a veteran of the Korean War. I may have lost my hair, but last time I looked, all my senses were present and accounted for."

He was getting agitated, so just to keep him calm Jamie agreed to do as he asked. If he wasn't better by dinner, however, she'd tell Gray.

Jamie was adding butter to a steaming pot of potatoes when Ivy, Halle, and Gray walked into the kitchen. Although they'd dropped their coats and boots in the mudroom, the clean, cold scent of the mountain still clung to them.

"Where's Dad?" Gray asked, setting his keys and wallet on the counter.

"Upstairs," Jamie replied, sticking a mixer into the pot. "Resting."

Gray frowned. "That isn't like him."

"Yeah, well. . ." The whirl of the beaters drowned out any further conversation, which was exactly what Jamie wanted. She watched the chunks of potato smooth and wondered if she should go back on her word to Norman. The decision was taken out of her hands a moment later when Jamie looked up and saw Norman in the doorway.

"Norman!" she said. "Glad you're feeling better."

"I was just about to explain to Gray here that the chili dog I had for lunch was talking to me." Norman gave her a slightly defiant look.

"You know chili dogs give you indigestion," Gray stated. "Why do you eat them?"

"Because they taste good."

Gray gave Norman a fond, but exasperated look. "You're impossible, Dad." He turned to Jamie. "You need any help?"

Jamie peeked at the chicken in the oven. "Nope. I'm all set. You've got about five minutes until dinner." She took off her apron and caught Gray's gaze lingering on her. There was a softness in his eyes she'd never seen before. He looked away quickly and left the room. Jamie stood still, watching the place he'd been. The heat of the oven warmed her back, but it couldn't account for the sudden heat in her cheeks or the breathless feeling that left her slightly light-headed and pleasantly tingly.

After dinner Norman asked if anyone wanted to play a board game.

"Which one?" Halle stacked two plates. "I kind of want to practice my instrument."

"Monopoly," Norman declared. "In honor of Jamie's profession."

"I don't know, Norman," Jamie said. "Maybe you should just take it easy. You barely ate anything."

"My digestion would benefit from a game of Monopoly," Norman stated firmly. Then in a much softer tone he added, "And maybe a little Mylanta."

After they cleaned the dishes and reset the dining room table for the breakfast buffet, all of them, including Boomer, marched into the family room.

"I want the dog piece," Halle declared, opening the playing board on the coffee table.

Jamie had never played Monopoly with Ivy before. They owned the game, but Jamie had always been either too busy or too tired to play. With a stab of guilt, she realized she should have made time. She hid the emotion under a confident smile. "You pick the next playing piece, sweetie."

Ivy rolled her eyes. "I'll be the Rolls-Royce."

"Jamie girl?" Norman prompted.

She picked up the first piece her hand fell on. "The iron." She pretended to iron her already perfectly straight hair. Halle laughed, but Ivy cringed.

"You be the shoe, Gray. I'll be the hat." Norman began handing out money.

"Hold on," Gray said. "I should be banker."

"Oh no. I'm always the banker." His father winked at Halle. "Maybe Halle should decide."

Halle grinned. "Grandpa is always banker, Dad."

Gray pretended to look crushed as he set the Chance and Community Chest cards on the board. "Okay," he said, "but I'm keeping a close eye on you, Dad." Then he grinned at Ivy. "You have to watch out for Mr. Westler—he cheats."

Ivy's eyes lit up, and she laughed.

"I don't cheat," Norman replied with dignity.

"You cheat, Dad," Gray said flatly. "Show me your sleeves."

Norman held out his arms for inspection. Halle and Ivy laughed as two five-hundred-dollar bills fell out of his sleeves. "Now how did those get there?" he asked innocently.

"My own father—a cheater." Gray sighed dramatically and almost, but not quite, hid a smile. "Tell you what, Dad. I'll let you get away with it this time, but the next time I catch you stealing from the bank you're going straight to jail."

"That's fine," Norman agreed. "Now let's get this game started before the next millennium comes."

Halle rolled the dice and the game began. By the time they'd all gone around the board a couple of times, Norman had talked Halle and Ivy into forming an alliance with him. Although Norman offered the same deal to Jamie, she turned to Gray and smiled. "How about making me a better offer?"

"Team with me and I'll give you another free ski lesson."

"That's not fair," Norman growled as Jamie shook Gray's hand.

"Sorry, Norman," Jamie said. "I need the lesson." It was more than that, but she kept this to herself.

After an hour, both sides were about equal. Norman's team had slightly more cash, but she and Gray had more properties.

"Gray," Norman said. "Would you mind getting me a glass of water from the kitchen?" He rubbed his stomach. "That chili dog is talking to me again."

"Jamie, please keep an eye on him," Gray warned and left the room.

"Jamie! Is that a mouse under that chair?" Norman pointed excitedly.

Jamie jerked her head around. She was terrified of anything that crawled. Fortunately, she didn't see any furry little rodent. "I think that's just a dust bunny." Something about the game board looked different—she didn't think all those extra houses on Norman's properties had been there before. Halle and Ivy were studiously not looking at her.

Despite the extra houses and a few properties that inexplicably ended in Norman's possession, Jamie and Grayson soon found themselves winning. When Halle landed on Park Place, which belonged to Jamie, it nearly bankrupted Norman's team.

"You want to concede?" Gray began slowly counting out the cash Halle handed him.

"What do you think, girls? Should we admit defeat?"

"Probably," Ivy said. "We've got less than two hundred dollars."

Jamie yawned and dropped one of the dice. She leaned over to pick it up and saw paper money lying near Norman's battered sheepskin slippers. "Hey, Norman," she said. "You must have dropped some money." She handed him two five-hundred-dollar bills.

"How did those get there?" Norman's brow furrowed.

"As if you didn't know," Grayson stated. "I wouldn't be surprised if you were sitting on several other five-hundred-dollar bills."

The girls laughed excitedly. Jamie couldn't get over the look on Ivy's face. She was glowing with happiness and looked about five years younger.

"I'm not sitting on anything," Norman declared. "You can check if you like."

"I will. Stand up, Dad."

Norman did. "See? Totally innocent. You should be ashamed, Gray, for thinking otherwise."

Gray snorted. "And I suppose Boomer hid that money when nobody was looking." He turned to Jamie. "Did my father hide that money there when I went to get his water?"

"Nope," Jamie said. "He put extra houses on the board when you got his water." She enjoyed the look of mock displeasure on Gray's face and the sound of the girls' laughter.

"Come on, Dad, fess up. You put the money there."

"I didn't." Norman shook his head. "I'm innocent."

"So who did?" He scrutinized each face, and when he looked at her, Jamie burst out in guilty laughter.

"My mom is a cheater!" But the way Ivy said it, it didn't sound like a bad thing.

"Sabotage," Gray declared, shaking his head. "I give up. You all win." He didn't sound unhappy, though, and his eyes sparkled at her.

Norman gave his teammates a high five, then he beamed at Jamie. "You're quite a gal, Jamie." He turned to his son. "Isn't she?"

Gray looked up from putting away the game pieces. "She's something," he agreed and winked at Jamie. She thought she saw something tender in his eyes, but whatever he had been about to say was lost as Mrs. Banbridge, one of the guests, rapped on the french doors and asked if Jamie had any pastries left over from the morning.

# seventeen

"Could I please have your recipe for the lemon blueberry muffins?" Mrs. Banbridge asked. Although it was barely six thirty in the morning, Mrs. Banbridge was in full makeup and dressed for the ski slopes. The older woman and her husband hadn't been the first at the table, either. Skiers, Jamie had discovered, were early risers. Well, the nonteenage ones, she amended.

Smiling, Jamie walked to the white-haired woman's side and replenished Mrs. Banbridge's cup with hot coffee. "Absolutely. It's not my recipe, though. It's my Aunt Bea's."

"If you're giving out recipes," Mr. Gregory said from the other end of the table, "please give my wife the one for that egg, cheese, and sausage casserole. You wouldn't have any left over from yesterday, would you?"

Jamie smiled at the wistful note in his voice. "I don't. But I'll make it tomorrow morning, and I'll be glad to give you the recipe." She raised her voice to address Mr. Banbridge who was hard of hearing. "More coffee, Mr. Banbridge? Gray says the weather's supposed to warm up this afternoon, so the skiing will be best earlier."

Mr. Banbridge held up his cup for a refill. "The powder's always best early." He gestured to his wife. "Hope it stays this good for the race on Saturday. Barbara and I are the oldest racers in the husband/wife race. We won it in 1975, you know."

"Only because Alice was eight months pregnant with Grayson and Norman wouldn't let her race." Mrs. Banbridge laughed. "How many years did Norman and Alice win that trophy?"

"At least ten," Mr. Banbridge said, pulling another muffin from the basket and cutting it open. "And then Gray and Lonna

109

got married and continued the family tradition." He popped a piece of muffin in his mouth.

"Those two were simply unbeatable," Mrs. Banbridge said. "It's no wonder Halle is so talented. With those genes for skiing, she'd have to be." She glanced around the room and added casually, "Terrible shame what happened to Lonna, though."

Jamie kept her head down. "What happened?"

"Car accident." Mrs. Banbridge lowered her voice. "She hit a patch of black ice on I-84 and the car spun out of control, straight into the path of an eighteen-wheeler. Killed her instantly." She glanced around the room again and added softly, "Some witnesses said she was driving too fast."

Jamie's mind struggled to process the information even as questions bubbled up in her. How long ago? Had she been alone? And Gray. Her heart ached for him. She realized Mrs. Banbridge was waiting for her to comment. "It must have been awful," Jamie murmured.

"Oh it was," Mrs. Banbridge said. "If it wasn't for that little girl, I think Gray would have died from his grief. Shut himself up in the house for weeks." Her gaze grew troubled. "Norman about lost his mind trying to keep everything together— running the ski hill, teaching Gray's classes, and keeping the B & B open. It got so bad they almost sold this place." She shook her head. "Got themselves a Realtor and all but signed the paperwork."

Jamie cringed, thinking how hard she had pushed Gray to let her list the ski hill. No wonder he'd nearly thrown her out of his office that first day. Her hands were shaking a little as she picked up a coffee mug. "Why didn't he? Why didn't he sell?"

Mrs. Banbridge shrugged. "I don't really know. Darren and I were so glad, we didn't press for more." She patted Jamie's hand. "I don't go around telling just anybody that story, you know. You probably think I'm a gossipy old woman with nothing better to do than talk about somebody else's business."

"I don't think that at all," Jamie protested. But she was

wondering why the older woman had decided to share the story with her.

Mrs. Banbridge gripped Jamie's arm with surprising strength. "I saw you all in the family room last night, playing Monopoly," the older woman said. "You were all laughing, and that dog was sleeping in front of the fire. I knew in my heart there was love there. There was a *family* there. Men don't always tell a woman the things she needs to know." She squeezed Jamie's arm. "Gray's special. Take good care of him. Now, do you use cream cheese in the recipe?"

Jamie was too stunned by Mrs. Banbridge's words and her own tangle of emotions to do anything but nod.

"Thought so," the old woman said and sipped her coffee with an unmistakable look of satisfaction stamped across her weathered features.

જ

Mrs. Banbridge had it all wrong. Gray and Jamie weren't in love, and there had been two families playing Monopoly last night, not one. Jamie clicked her bindings into place and propelled herself toward the double chairlift. Her heart tugged, however, at the memory of all of them clustered around the coffee table in the family room, talking and laughing. She hadn't seen Ivy look so happy for a long time.

*What if the thing Ivy needed most was a family? Gray's family?* She imagined family game nights, long walks in the woods, and holidays with the big dining room table filled with people. *Hold on,* she warned herself. *Aren't you getting a little ahead of yourself? If you want to give Ivy a happy future, maybe you should be thinking about how you're going to pay her tuition at Miss Porter's.* She plunked herself down on the chairlift and tried to think about her job. She'd been neglecting it lately and resolved to check her messages more frequently as well as check new listings on the MLS.

At the top of the mountain, she headed for Mad Hatter. As usual, the trail was nearly empty. When she reached the trailhead, she paused, watching a few skiers and a lone snow-boarder gracefully slide out of sight. She took a deep breath.

*Are you there?* She listened carefully to the white silence. *Can you hear me?* Not even a squirrel moved through the woods. *Idiot,* she thought, *who did you think was going to answer—God? And even if He did, what did you think He'd say? Hey, Jamie, great to see you. Let's talk.* She gripped her ski poles more tightly. No. If God were going to talk to her, He'd probably say something like, *Why didn't you listen to me? Why did you get into Devon Brown's Mustang that night? We both know I tried to stop you. I was the fear in your stomach, the dryness of your mouth, the crushing beat of your heart.*

"Stop it!" she cried. "How could I ever regret having Ivy?" Her voice rang out in the quiet forest. She was ashamed and fearful that someone might have overheard. She listened hard. In the distance she heard voices—but they weren't God's. Other skiers were approaching, and she didn't want to be seen standing at the top of the trail talking to herself. She pushed off, wanting to get away from her thoughts, away from the faint hope that God would hear the need in her heart.

At the bottom of the mountain, she spotted Ivy heading toward the double chairlift and hurried to catch up to her. "Hey," she called. "Wait up."

Ivy obediently paused long enough for Jamie to reach her.

"How's it going?"

"Fine."

"Where's Halle?"

"Back at the house practicing her french horn." Ivy crinkled her nose. "Mr. Grayson told her to practice when the guests weren't around."

Jamie made a sympathetic noise. "When I was in fifth grade, I wanted to play the clarinet. I squeaked that instrument so badly my mom made me practice in the basement with the door closed." She bit her lip. It only made things worse for Ivy to hear about the family that had never acknowledged her.

"You think your mother ever thinks about us?"

"I don't know. Maybe." Jamie inched her skis forward in the lift line, thinking she'd asked herself that same question hundreds of times.

"You think I'll ever meet either of your parents?"

Something in Ivy's voice made Jamie glance at her. Her stomach tightened at the barely disguised longing on her daughter's face. "Ivy, you know I really don't like to talk about my family."

"It's my family, too," Ivy stated, but her voice lacked conviction. "Maybe we should visit them sometime. You know, just show up at their doorstep."

Jamie shuddered. She remembered showing up at her parents' house uninvited with three-month-old Ivy in her arms. Her mother had backed away from the door with her hands pressed to her mouth, while Jamie stood on the welcome mat like a stranger. Her father, finally, had come to the door. He'd had a check in his hand and a pinched look to his mouth. Understanding just what that check represented, Jamie hadn't wanted to take it, but she'd needed the money. By then Aunt Bea was in hospice, and the bills had been accumulating. Jamie remembered the door closing and the sound of the lock snapping into place. Fortunately, Ivy would never remember that day. "I don't think so," she said very gently.

The chairlift swung around the turn. Two people took their seats, and as their chair lifted them into the air, Jamie and Ivy poled forward to catch the next one. A moment later they were seated and the chair was ascending the mountain.

"Are they so terrible?" Ivy asked. "How do you know they wouldn't be happy to see me?" She flipped her long, sleek ponytail. "I happen to be smart and good looking."

"You are," Jamie agreed, smiling, but beneath her daughter's bravado, she sensed a deep insecurity. "It's not anything about the way you look or anything you've done." Jamie hesitated. They'd gone over this more than once, but each time Ivy was less content with her answers. "Look, they're not awful. They just want their lives to run a certain way."

"We wouldn't try and run their lives." Ivy shot her a look packed with emotion. "I wouldn't, at least."

Jamie ignored the barb. She watched the skiers moving gracefully down the hill beneath the lift line. "Trust me, Ivy. We're better off without them."

"I'm the only girl at Miss Porter's who doesn't have siblings, a father, grandparents, stepparents. . .cousins. . .anything." She scowled fiercely at Jamie. "I'm like an alien."

Jamie shook her head. "You're not an alien." More softly she added, "And you've got me."

"You shut me down every time I ask about my father or your family." Bitterness and resignation hung in the air like frosty breath.

*Because I'm trying to protect you.* Jamie's cheeks burned despite the cold air. "I love you, Ivy. I've done what I thought was right."

They were close to the mountain, and Jamie knew time was running out. "Hey, listen," she said. "I've been wanting to talk to you about the club race. I've spoken to Gray, and he's agreed to let us join the Pilgrim's Peak race team so you and I can go in the mother/daughter race this Saturday." She gave Ivy a big smile. "I've been practicing, and I think we can make a decent showing."

Ivy shifted on the seat. "You're kidding, right?"

"I think it'd be fun." She gave Ivy the encouraging smile she used on her most reluctant clients.

"I don't think so," Ivy said.

"Why not? I've been practicing, and there was only one time I missed a gate. I won't be the best skier out there, but I won't embarrass you."

The sign instructing skiers to raise the safety bar flashed past them. "Because I don't want to. That's why."

"How about we ski down the race trail together and then

we talk about this some more?" Jamie kept her gaze on Ivy's unrelenting profile. "You'll see how much better I've gotten. I can even get off the chairlift now." She was joking, of course, but Ivy didn't laugh or smile or even roll her eyes.

"Mom," Ivy said sharply. "Why don't you ever listen to what I want?"

The skiers in front of them were unloading, and there was no time to answer. Ivy took off the minute her skis hit the packed snow. She immediately headed down the trail, her slender body tucked for speed. Jamie could only watch her go, filled with the sad realization that whatever was broken between them might be beyond her ability to fix.

# eighteen

"Jamie," Gray yelled. "Slow down!" What was wrong with her today? She was skiing faster than usual—almost recklessly. She'd wiped out a couple of times already, and it hadn't slowed her down one bit. She maneuvered a gate, taking it at an angle that would have been impressive if he'd had any faith at all that she was in control.

In the next instant, it happened. She hooked a ski on the inside of the gate. The pole gave, but not before it knocked her off balance. Both bindings popped, and she crashed to the ground.

An adrenaline rush shot through his body. Before he even thought about it, he launched himself uphill. Her bindings had released, but people broke bones or tore tendons in their knees all the time. His heart thumped. "Jamie!"

She sat up slowly and began brushing snow from her parka. "I'm okay," she said but winced when she said it.

He continued to sidestep up the hill as quickly as he could. "Don't move until I get there," he ordered.

When he reached her side, he scanned her for any sign of injury. Other than a pretty good amount of snow clinging to her clothing and her hair, she looked fine. Suddenly it was much easier to breathe. "What were you thinking?" He helped her to her feet and brushed some snow from her parka. "Didn't you hear me tell you to slow down?"

"I thought I could do it."

"You thought you could do it?" Gray slapped at the snow a little harder than necessary, but he couldn't seem to help himself. "Do you realize if your binding hadn't popped quickly enough, you'd be looking at a spiral fracture?"

"Fortunately, I'm fine," Jamie snapped. "Stop being a worrywart."

"I'll stop being a worrywart when you start showing some common sense." Gray glared down at her, thinking he'd like to shake some sense into her.

"You don't like my skiing, don't watch." Her eyes flashed defiance.

He set his jaw. If she wanted a fight, she'd get one. "Fine," he said. "I'm pulling your ticket. You don't listen, and I'm not going to stand here and watch you get hurt. That wasn't part of our deal."

"Fine," she snapped. "It's what you wanted anyway."

"Is isn't what I wanted." He slid a few feet backward and was about to swing his skis around when he thought he saw her face crumple. It occurred to him through his haze of anger that she was about to cry. "Jamie?"

"Keep going!" she thundered. "Just like everyone else."

"I'm not like everyone else!" he yelled back and began to sidestep back up the hill. She saw him coming and tried to put her skis back on, but there was snow under one of the bindings. She stepped harder and harder onto the back of the binding, but it refused to close.

"You want to tell me what's going on?" He felt some of his anger evaporating at the sight of her waling on the poor ski.

"I'm done," Jamie snapped. She gave up on the ski and started to walk away. Her boots punched holes into the snow.

He grabbed her arm. "We have one disagreement, and you're done? I thought there was more to you than that."

"You were wrong." She tried to shrug off his grasp, but he tightened his fingers. "Let go of me!"

"Not until I understand what's going on."

"I told you. I'm quitting the race."

"Half the ski hill heard that, but I'm still waiting to hear why."

"It doesn't matter."

"It matters to me."

Someone uphill yelled for them to clear the course. Gray scooped up Jamie's skis and sidestepped to the side. She trailed behind him silently, and when he glanced over his shoulder, he saw the uncharacteristic slump of her shoulders.

They'd barely reached the edge of the trail when a group of snowboarders sped through the gates. He heard the edges of their boards slice through the snow, but kept his gaze on Jamie's face. She was doing it again. Melting some part of him that warned him not to get too involved. Maybe it was his sanity. He didn't understand how one minute he'd be furious with her, and now all he wanted to do was take her into his arms. "Just for the record," he said, "I'm pulling your lift ticket, not walking away from you."

She glanced up, surprise in her eyes. "Yes you were. You were skiing backward down the hill and picking up speed."

"That was before," Gray said. "I'm not moving now. I'm very stationary. It'd probably take a Sno-Cat to move me right now."

She made a sound that could have been either a laugh or a cry. He touched her arm, and she turned toward him, searching his eyes and looking more miserable than he could ever remember seeing her.

"I'm sorry," she said at last. "You're right. I was being reckless. I just didn't care if I got hurt or not."

"Well, I do."

"Ivy and I had an argument," Jamie admitted. "She hated the idea of the mother/daughter race." She laughed a little bitterly. "She can't wait to go back to Miss Porter's and get away from me."

"She's a teenager," Gray stated. "She doesn't really know what she wants."

Jamie shook her head. "My whole life I've tried to give her the best of everything so she'd feel good about herself and not miss having a dad." She hesitated. "I can't do that anymore, Gray. I'm not even sure I can afford to keep her at Miss Porter's." She looked at him, and his heart ached at the despair in her eyes. "She hates me, Gray. I thought this mother/daughter race would help bring us together, but obviously it isn't going to happen. I've tried everything in my power, and it hasn't worked." She paused. "I don't know what else to do."

Gray remembered when Lonna died. He'd been overwhelmed by even the smallest decision, and his grief had been crushing, as if he were lying under a boulder and could barely draw a breath. He remembered crying out to God, begging him for the strength to love Halle when everything inside felt broken. "Talk to God, Jamie. I know He can help."

"I don't think God wants anything to do with me."

"What makes you say that?"

Jamie's gaze followed another group of skiers speeding down the slope. "There was a time in my life when I really needed Him and He wasn't there."

"Maybe He was, but you couldn't see it."

Jamie's lips tightened. "I don't think so."

"When Lonna died, I wanted to be angry with Him and to blame Him," Gray admitted. "Every time I looked at Halle, I thought about all the things Lonna would never see—Halle's first date, Halle's graduation from high school, what college she'd go to, what she would look like on her wedding day. The face of our first grandchild." He felt himself teeter on the edge of something dark and painful and pushed forward. "It was like I was dead on the inside, Jamie, and there was nothing for me to give anyone. Not God, not my father—not even Halle. I couldn't let her grow up that way. I knew I had a choice—to stay angry at God and turn from Him, or I could turn to Him." He sighed. "He helped me put my life back together, and He can help you do the same. Whatever you've done, Jamie, it isn't greater than His love for you."

❧

*Whatever you've done, Jamie, it isn't greater than His love for you.* Gray's words continued to resonate in her mind. She barely tasted the pizza Gray had had delivered and skipped dessert entirely, preferring to escape to her room. Standing by the darkened window, she looked blankly into the night and thought about what Gray had said about faith. When Ivy came into the room, Jamie found their silence unbearable and took refuge in a long shower. Even with the water pounding over her, she found herself wondering what her life would have been like if she'd turned to God instead of running away from Him. Would it have made a difference? And if so, could it make a difference now?

She put on her pajamas and bathrobe and wound her long hair into a towel.

In the bedroom, Ivy lay under the covers listening to her iPod. "Ivy, can I talk to you?"

No reply. Jamie reached over and unplugged Ivy's ears. "Can we talk, please?"

Ivy shrugged. "Whatever."

Jamie released a breath she hadn't known she was holding. She studied her daughter's full lips, so reminiscent of Devon's, and her large blue eyes, the mirror of her own. "We need to talk about this afternoon," she began.

Ivy pulled her knees up, turning the comforter into a tent. She looked ready to disappear into the folds of the covers at any second. *It's no use*, Jamie thought. *She hates me. This is hopeless.*

*Just ask God.* Jamie could almost hear Gray's deep voice urging her not to be afraid. She feared it was hopeless, and yet something insisted she try. She closed her eyes. *If You can hear me, I need Your help to reach my daughter. And if You don't want to do it for me, please do it for Ivy. She's blameless in all this.*

"I know you don't want to go in the mother/daughter race," Jamie said. "I'm not going to fight you on that. But something you said to me on the chairlift really bothered me. You said I never listen to what you want. Is that how you really feel?"

Ivy pleated the top edge of the comforter and avoided Jamie's gaze. "Yeah."

"But I give you everything you want," Jamie said.

"Just forget it. Whenever I try and talk to you, all you do is tell me why I'm wrong."

Jamie mentally counted to ten. "I'm sorry. Let's try it again."

"Oh, what's the point?" Ivy asked bitterly. "You really don't care."

"Of course I do." Jamie's stomach tightened into a hard lump. Just as she'd feared, God wasn't going to help her. Ivy had made up her mind to leave her—just like Devon and her parents had so many years ago. It was only a matter of time. She steadied the towel wrapped around her wet hair. She wanted—no needed—to look at her face in the mirror and see if there was anything visible that would explain just what it was about her that was so unacceptable. So unlovable.

"Okay," Ivy said. "I wanted to go to Aspen for Christmas. First you said yes, then you said no. I think you only wanted me to come to Connecticut so you wouldn't look like a bad parent to Mr. Grayson."

Jamie's hand went to her mouth. "Oh no, honey. Never that. I told you, it was the money thing. The Coleman sale fell through, and I couldn't swing it."

Ivy's eyes flashed. "You managed to swing diamond earrings for me for Christmas."

Jamie's hands automatically went to her earlobes, although she'd taken out the studs before she'd showered. She took a breath, hating what needed to be said next. "I gave you my diamond studs and bought myself a pair of cubic zirconias so no one would know."

Ivy seemed to shrink as the realization sank in. "But Mom. You love those earrings. I remember how proud you were when you bought them."

"I love you more," Jamie stated. "And I wanted you to have a really great Christmas gift. I still do. As soon as I can swing it, we'll pick out something more your taste."

Ivy shook her head. "No. It's okay. I didn't know. I thought you wanted me to look exactly like you. To be your clone."

Jamie winced at the choice of words. "I don't want you to be anything but my daughter."

"That's the trouble," Ivy said sadly. "I'm not just your daughter. I have a father and grandparents and who knows, maybe aunts and uncles and cousins." Her voice thickened as she visibly struggled to keep control of herself. "Why can't you tell me about them? Aren't I good enough for them?"

Jamie placed her hand on the tent pole that was Ivy's knee and felt the bony contour through the thick comforter. *What words, God? What words? If I say the wrong ones, I'll just make things worse.* "You're better than all of them put together." Jamie drew a shaky breath. "I don't like to talk about them because I don't want you to know them. They'll only hurt you, Ivy, just like they did me."

"Whatever happened," Ivy said flatly, "I want to know. I want to stop wondering if my dad is a secret agent or if we're in the witness protection program."

"We're not in the witness protection program, and your dad is not a spy—at least he wasn't when I knew him."

"Then who was he? What did he look like?" Ivy's voice cracked a bit. "I want to know his full name—and if he knew about me. If he ever saw me or. . .held me."

Jamie looked away from the vulnerability in her daughter's eyes. How much of the truth could Ivy handle? Her gaze moved to the brass door handle. Everything inside wanted to bolt out the door, run into the night and away from this conversation. She gripped her cold hands together. *I can't give her what she needs, God.*

Her gaze returned to Ivy, who was watching her intently. Jamie feared the judgment in those eyes. She wasn't prepared for the compassion in her daughter's voice as Ivy lifted the down comforter as much as Jamie's presence on the bed would allow. "You're shaking, Mom. It's warmer under the covers."

Jamie crawled into the bed. She heard the radiator's hiss and felt the heat coming off Ivy's body. When Ivy was a baby, the two of them used to cuddle in bed like this, keeping each other warm through the long Maine winter.

What Ivy needed to hear didn't start there, though. Jamie wound Ivy's hair around her index finger and began the story her daughter had waited thirteen years to hear.

# nineteen

Jamie was serving breakfast in the dining room the next morning when Ivy walked in. It was just after six and way earlier than her daughter usually made an appearance. "Is everything okay?"

Ivy nodded, muttered a nearly incoherent good morning to the guests, and grabbed a lemon cheesecake muffin with the crumble topping. Jamie pretended not to notice her daughter's gaze following her as she moved about the room. When she went into the kitchen to refill the coffeepot, Ivy followed her.

"Look," Ivy said to Jamie's back. "I've been thinking. If it really means a lot to you for us to enter the mother/daughter race, I'll do it."

Jamie nearly dropped the coffeepot. She composed her face before she turned. "Only if you really want to do it." She realized immediately Ivy was wearing the diamond earrings. Her breath caught in her chest. Instinct, however, warned her to play it cool.

"Whatever," Ivy said and began to pick apart the muffin with her fingers. "If you want, maybe we could practice on the course this afternoon. I could give you some pointers."

With her free hand Jamie picked up a recipe card she had begun writing earlier that morning and slipped it into the pocket of her apron. She hoped Ivy didn't see how hard her hand was shaking. "Okay," she said. "I'll be ready to go about nine o'clock."

After Ivy left, Jamie leaned against the counters. Had her daughter actually suggested they spend some time together? She closed her eyes. *Thank You,* she said. *Now please help me not to blow it.*

124

She heard Gray's voice coming from the dining room. Opening her eyes, she set the coffeepot down and hurried out of the kitchen. She couldn't wait to give him the exciting news.

৵

Gray was thrilled to hear Ivy had decided to partner with Jamie in the mother/daughter race. He was less thrilled with Halle, who was late to practice later that afternoon. He searched the top of the mountain for her. With the interclub race just days away, every moment of practice time was valuable. Besides, it wasn't fair to the other kids who were waiting to get started.

"Sorry, Dad," Halle said, shushing to a stop just inches from the tips of his skis. "I was practicing scales."

"I don't want to hear any excuses," Gray said coldly and watched the sparkle die in his daughter's eyes. He ignored the urge to say something encouraging to her. "Today we're practicing our starts." He climbed up the snowy start gate he'd created and demonstrated how the kids should do it. "Just like that." He gestured to the tall, lanky teenager next to him. "You try it, Chris."

The boy took his place at the top of the embankment Gray had created with the Sno-Cat. Chris began to slide back and forth as Gray began the countdown.

"Great," he yelled as the boy sped out of the makeshift gate.

He let all the other kids go, but held Halle back. Watching her take her place in the starting gate, he remained silent. She signaled her readiness, but Gray couldn't start the countdown. *Did you know, Halle,* he wanted to say, *that your mother once dreamed about trying out for the US ski team? But then she had you—and she gave up those dreams because she didn't want to leave you. She never complained, not once, but I knew deep inside there was a part of her that wondered what could have been. She used to hold you off the ground and swing you gently side to side, like you were skiing. This is our Olympic baby, she'd say. Our gold-medal girl.*

"Dad?" Halle prompted.

He looked at his daughter and saw Lonna's face at that age. Young, strong, bursting with confidence and desire to show the world just how good she was. Lonna whispering dreams about the mountains they'd ski and the races they'd win. Lonna laughing as he warned her to be careful the snowy afternoon she'd gone out to buy Halle's favorite cookies—Social Tea Biscuits—for a make-believe tea party. Lonna pale and still beautiful in the clothing he'd picked out for her funeral service.

"Halle," he started and then didn't quite know what to say.

"I'm really sorry about being late, Dad. It won't happen again."

"I know," he said. "You ready?"

She nodded.

"Okay, then." He counted down and watched her launch herself out of the starting gate. She flashed past him in a tight tuck, and he watched her back grow smaller as she sped down the hill.

Gray braced himself against a piercing, cold gust. The wind was always strongest on this part of the mountain. Harder to handle was the thought that the dreams he'd held on to so tightly might be long gone, and if he opened his fingers he'd find his hands were as empty as those of a magician who had successfully performed a disappearing coin trick.

New Year's Eve arrived on the heels of some uncharacteristically warm weather. Despite his best efforts, Gray watched the sun erode the snow base, and patches of straggly grass and mud appeared in the places worn thin by skiers. Business dropped off, especially when he had to close several trails in order to concentrate his snow-making efforts on the main ones. Gray couldn't stop thinking how one bad year had put Powder Ridge out of business. The thought of seeing Pilgrim's Peak on the auction block haunted him.

The rain began falling lightly at dusk. Gray was in no mood for the party, which already was in full swing when he walked into the family room. Norman stuck a silly hat on him and pulled him toward the front of the room. "We're playing charades," he said. "Hurry up, Gray. Our team could use you. The theme is movies, and Jamie's team is killing us."

Gray shrugged off his father's arm. It was supposed to rain all night and all the next day. Then, if this wasn't bad enough, the temperature was supposed to drop below freezing tomorrow night. The hill was going to be like skiing down a glacier. "No thanks, Dad," he said. He picked a slice of pizza off the buffet table.

"Window!" Jamie shouted. *"Rear Window!"*

Gray felt a draft of air. It was coming from a window Mrs. Banbridge had cracked open. She appeared to be shooing something through the narrow opening. Her team seated on the couch had fallen into speculative silence.

"Fire!" Mrs. Gregory finally yelled. *"Towering Inferno!"*

Mrs. Banbridge shook her head and opened the window wider.

"I think she's trying to climb out the window," Mr. Gregory stated. He pulled his moustache. *"Escape from Alcatraz,"* he shouted.

Gray grinned as Mrs. Banbridge pretended the cold air coming in from the window was powerful enough to knock her backward. She struggled against an invisible wind that was trying to blow her backward. *"Ghost,"* Halle shouted.

*"The Mist,"* Ivy yelled.

Mrs. Banbridge stopped struggling against the wind and started laughing. After a moment she walked over to the draperies and wrapped one around herself. *"The Mummy,"* Jamie called out. Ivy and Halle burst out laughing.

As Mrs. Banbridge pantomimed throwing random things out the window, Gray's gaze traveled to the back of the couch. Jamie's long, sleek ponytail bobbed with laughter as Mrs. Banbridge lost her grip on a plastic cup and sent it sailing into the darkness.

Crossing the room, he stopped in front of the couch and told

Halle to scoot over a bit. Seating himself next to Jamie, Gray established himself as part of their team. A log popped in the fireplace, and Mrs. Banbridge resumed waving at everybody as Dr. Goldman, who was on the other team, gave them a five-second warning.

"*Gone with the Wind,*" Gray yelled, as surprised as anyone else to find the words coming from him.

Mrs. Banbridge nodded and beamed at him as the other team good-naturedly protested his involvement. Gray glanced sideways at Jamie, who was smiling in delight at him.

She was warm and soft against his side, and she smelled like cinnamon. Something deep inside him started to relax. The sound of the rain disappeared in the voices as Mr. Gregory took his turn in front of the fireplace. Gray looked into Jamie's face, and suddenly the New Year was filled with possibilities he would never have imagined existed a month ago.

# twenty

A light rain continued to fall on New Year's Day. Jamie stayed inside and thought she'd lose her mind with Ivy peppering questions at her. Why couldn't they drive down to Greenwich and drop in on her parents? Could Ivy call them herself and then hang up when they answered? Could Jamie give Ivy her credit card number so Ivy could hire an Internet service that would help her locate Devon?

Jamie stayed busy in the kitchen, answering with monosyllables—mostly noes—and reminding Ivy that the interclub race was the next day and that she couldn't very well leave Gray and Norman to do all the work.

"You're putting me off again," Ivy stated.

"And you're getting on my nerves." Jamie smashed an egg against the side of the bowl so hard the yolk dripped down the outside edge. "I told you, you've got to give me time to figure things out."

"You've had thirteen years to figure it out," Ivy said. "I can't wait any longer."

Jamie pushed back a strand of hair and met her daughter's determined gaze. "You have to wait until after the interclub race."

"You promise?"

"Only if you understand they might not be the grandparents you want."

Ivy held out her hand. "Deal."

After lunch, when the rain finally stopped, Jamie escaped to Pilgrim's Peak with Norman. They carried boxes of office supplies toward the lodge. "Careful," Jamie warned. The temperature was dropping, and already she could feel a thin layer of ice forming in the parking lot. She glanced uneasily at the glassy coating on the limbs of trees and power lines. "Will we still be able to have the ski race tomorrow?"

"Oh sure," Norman said, picking his way over the semi-frozen ground. "Gray'll break up the ice on the mountain with the Sno-Cat. The hill will be fast," he warned in his gravelly voice, "but it won't stop anyone from coming."

His prediction turned out to be completely accurate. Despite icy roads and frigid weather, by seven o'clock the next morning the ski lodge was packed. Jamie could hardly hear herself think in the low roar of voices. She handed out dozens of numbered racing bibs as Norman provided a running commentary on the PA system.

A few hours later, new volunteers arrived to give Jamie and Norman a break. Although Norman refused to give up the microphone, he urged Jamie to find a good spot on Alice's Alley to watch the races. "If you hurry," he explained, "you'll be in time to see Ivy and Halle."

Jamie hurried to the chairlift. As it carried her up the mountain, she heard the crowd cheer each time a skier completed the course. Norman's voice boomed out the time. When she dismounted at the top, she hurried to Alice's Alley.

Gray had warned her about the corn snow—the little nubs of ice that had been formed by the Sno-Cat—but Jamie hadn't realized just how hard it would be to turn and control her speed. She found herself struggling with her wedge turns and nearly skiing into another spectator as she sought free space along the orange safety net.

A girl in a silver bodysuit and bowl-shaped helmet flashed past. Jamie heard the girl's skis hiss across the ice as she maneuvered around a gate.

Jamie's cold hands tightened into fists as racer after racer sped through the course. There were a few wipeouts, one poor child missed a gate, and another had a false start. Her heart began to race when she spotted her daughter at the top of the hill.

"Go, Ivy," Jamie murmured as her gaze followed her daughter. "Go, Ivy," she said more loudly as Ivy picked up speed. "Go, Ivy!" Jamie screamed at the top of her lungs as her daughter neared, then blasted past. Ivy finished the final turn and held a tight tuck as she crossed under the finish line.

Then Halle was coming down the course at full speed. Jamie had never seen her ski full-out. Even knowing as little as she did about skiing, she could tell Halle was in a class by herself. Smooth and graceful, her skis barely seemed to touch the snow.

"Go, Halle!" Jamie bellowed as the girl rocketed past her. Unable to stay where she was for a second longer, Jamie skied down the rest of the mountain. She found Halle and Ivy among the crowd of spectators and competitors milling about the finish line. The girls were hugging each other and jumping up and down.

"Ivy's had the best time so far!" Halle cried out when she saw Jamie.

Ivy had beaten Halle? She looked at her daughter's face for confirmation. "Only by, like, a tenth of a second," Ivy said, trying and failing to appear as if this were no big deal.

"We're in first and second place!" both girls said in unison.

Jamie opened her arms. "Girls, I am so proud of you both." They were as tall as Jamie, and yet both their heads folded into her neck as if they were much smaller and younger.

"Okay, Mom," Ivy said, drawing back. "Halle and I want to watch the rest of the junior race."

The two girls disappeared into the crowd. Jamie brought Norman a hot chocolate and a pastry. He seemed in good spirits and brushed off her offer to help. "Just go have fun," he said. "But be careful."

Jamie went back outside to watch the rest of the junior team races. The girls' race continued for another hour, but Ivy's and Halle's times held. Two other girls on their team also had good times, and by lunch Norman was announcing that the Pilgrim's

Peak junior girls had won their division. Jamie couldn't wait to see Gray's face.

Before she knew it, it was midafternoon and time for the mother/daughter race. Jamie rode the lift to the top of the hill with Ivy, who could not seem to sit still on the bench seat. "Don't worry about going fast on the course," Ivy coached. "My time will more than make up for yours. Just don't DQ."

Jamie knew DQ meant disqualify. "Don't worry," Jamie said. "If I have to slide on my back to the finish line, I will."

"Gate eight is the worst," Ivy said. "It's the one closest to the safety net, so you have to turn pretty sharply—and there's a lot of ice around it. You'll probably want to slow down before that gate."

"Right," Jamie agreed.

"Remember, Mom, after the last gate the race isn't finished. You should go into a low tuck until you cross the finish line. Races are won or lost in a hundredth of a second."

"Okay." Jamie smiled. Ivy was really into this racing thing. Just as she'd hoped, it was bringing them together. "This is fun, huh?"

"Yeah," Ivy agreed. "I've been thinking. You know how you said you wanted to wait until you weren't broke to introduce me to my grandparents? Well, if we won the race together, you would feel more confident and I wouldn't have to wait for you to start selling houses again."

The thought was so awful it was almost funny. She pictured both of them standing outside her parents' front door. "Hello," Jamie would say when one of them answered the bell. "This is for you." And she'd hand them an enormous golden trophy. "Can we be part of your life again?"

They'd nearly reached the top of the mountain, so Jamie lifted the safety bar. "Let's just get through this race."

The wind seemed to slice right through Jamie's parka as she and Ivy skied to the start of Alice's Alley. Over the heads of racers she spotted Gray at the starting gate. He had his arm raised like a flag and was about to send the next racer down the course. His face looked red and chapped from the extreme cold.

There were about twelve teams in the mother/daughter race. They ranged in size and shape, but most of them had skin-tight racing suits that said they'd done this before. Jamie looked at the grooves cut into the snow by the other skiers and felt slightly sick. None of the other skiers looked like they struggled with wedge turns.

Soon Gray called Ivy's number. Jamie gave her daughter a quick hug for luck, and almost immediately she was watching the back of her daughter speed down the hill. The crowd cheered and cowbells rang as Ivy leaned hard into the first gate.

When it was Jamie's turn, she lined up at the starting gate. Her heart was going full tilt, and her legs shook. Gray raised his arm. "Jamie? You ready?"

Jamie swallowed. The hill suddenly looked a lot steeper. She glanced at Gray and saw the tight, worried line of his mouth. She didn't trust herself to speak, so she just nodded.

He spoke into a radio and then began to count down. "Three . . .two. . .one. . . Go!"

Jamie hurled her body forward. At the same time, the wind gusted, pushing her forward. In the blink of an eye, she went from standstill to full speed. The crowd yelled encouragement as she headed for the first gate.

*Easy,* she cautioned herself as she flew down the icy course. The snow felt like hard little balls of packed ice under her skis. Cold air slashed her cheeks. Even behind the protective shield of her helmet, her eyes began to tear. She reached the first set of gates and aimed for the second. They came up quickly.

She swung a little wide after the second gate, but corrected herself in time to take the third, fourth, and fifth gates. She'd never skied so fast in her life, and it was both exhilarating and terrifying. More of the course flashed under her skis. She made no effort to check her speed. She'd either finish the course or crash. And then she glimpsed the eighth set of gates. They were straddling a large patch of ice.

Her skis made a shrill *sssssss* sound. She felt her downhill ski begin to skid out from under her. She threw her arms up for balance. She hit the side of the plastic gate, and her ski poles flew out of her hands. *Oh, God,* she screamed in her head. *Help me.* She braced herself for a fall that didn't come. Instead, somehow she remained balanced—one leg in the air and arms straight out to the side—and then miraculously she was off the ice and heading straight for the next set of gates.

She cut the next turns as tightly as she dared. Several times her skis chattered over icy chunks of snow, and once she came scarily close to the orange safety net holding back the spectators. But then the finish line was in sight, and she was streaking toward it, crouched over just like Ivy had instructed, and then she flashed under it. She straightened and forced her tired legs into a snowplow position before she plowed into the safety net.

Halle and Ivy rushed out to congratulate her. Both girls enveloped her in hugs as she struggled to catch her breath.

"Mom!" Ivy cried. "I can't believe how fast you went!"

"That makes two of us," Jamie panted. "I was never so scared in my life."

"You scared me, too, Miss Jamie."

"Gate eight," Jamie said. "I don't know what happened."

"You looked like you were doing this really weird yoga pose," Ivy declared, hugging her. "I seriously thought you were going to crash, but you didn't! You're amazing!"

Jamie realized she was still shaking from head to foot. Norman's voice came over the loudspeaker. "Ladies and gentlemen," he said. His voice shook with excitement. "I'm pleased to announce a blistering time of one minute two seconds!"

"That's the fastest mom's time yet!" Halle began to jump up and down. "And since Ivy had the fastest daughter time, you guys may be the winners!"

Jamie glanced at Ivy's glowing eyes and small but proud smile. It was worth that nerve-racking run down the mountain to see her daughter looking at her like that. A man she didn't recognize handed her her ski poles, and she smiled her thanks.

They moved aside as another racer sped across the finish line. A muscular woman in a blue and red racing suit hooted with laughter. "That was insane," she said. "And so much fun!" A chunky girl with a striped hat and scarf rushed out to give her a hug. Jamie watched the two embrace and smiled. Nothing like the fear of crashing on an icy slalom course to bring people together.

She waited for Norman to announce the woman's time. It seemed to be taking longer than usual, and she wondered if there had been some kind of complication. The silence stretched on and on. People began to murmur and look around. Jamie turned to Halle, who shrugged. "Maybe there's something wrong with the speaker system," she suggested.

Jamie nodded. That made sense. But then an unfamiliar voice boomed over the loudspeaker. "EMTs to the announcer's booth immediately!"

# twenty-one

Gray prayed. Jamie drove. When she pulled up in front of the emergency room at the Waterbury Hospital, he barely waited for the car to stop before jumping out. Pushing open the sliding double doors, he ran to the front desk.

"I'm looking for my father, Norman Westler. He came by ambulance. Probably arrived about a half hour ago."

"Let me see." A heavyset woman with black hair scraped into a painfully tight bun hit a few keys on a laptop computer. "He's in exam room three. I'll show you."

Gray followed the woman down a hallway lined with curtained-off examination rooms. He found his father lying on a bed with all sorts of electrodes hooked to his chest and an IV snaking out of his arm. His father's face was ashen.

"Dad." Gray reached his father's side in two steps. He peered into Norman's red-rimmed eyes, which looked painfully exposed without the thick lenses of his glasses. "What happened?"

"It was like an elephant was sitting on my chest," Norman replied, sounding subdued, but nonetheless alive and kicking. "And it hurt so bad I passed out. The next thing I knew the paramedics were strapping me to a stretcher."

A young man with a long skinny black braid walked into the examination area. "I'm Henry," he said to Gray, but his eyes were taking in the numbers on the monitors and he had a needle and syringe in his hands. "I'm the nurse helping to care for Mr. Westler."

"I'm his son, Grayson Westler. What's going on?"

"He's already had some nitroglycerin, and now I'm giving your father a shot of morphine. It'll help with the pain and with the workload on his heart."

"His heart?" Gray felt his own skip a couple of beats. "You think he's had a heart attack?"

"The doctor will want to talk to you about that." He turned to Norman. "How are you feeling, Mr. Westler?"

"Like I never should have had that chili dog at lunch."

Henry laughed, but his brown eyes were serious. "What time did you eat?"

"About noon."

Gray rolled a stool closer to the bed and sat near his father's head. If Henry was asking about the food his dad had eaten, he was probably thinking surgery. *Oh, God,* he thought. *No.* "He probably had at least two chili dogs," Gray added. "And french fries and a soda. Maybe a chocolate pudding."

"It was an ice-cream sandwich," Norman corrected. "And a pastry."

"I'll let the doctor know." Henry left the room.

Gray stared down at his father's shiny bald head. He hoped it was the fluorescent lights that painted an unhealthy cast to his dad's skin color. He tried to warm his dad's cold fingers, but his own were barely warmer. "You're going to be okay, Dad. They're going to take good care of you here."

"I'm not afraid to die." A look of pain crossed his features. "If it's my time, I'm ready to go to Jesus."

Gray rubbed his dad's hand gently. "You're not going to Jesus today."

"How do you know?"

"You're still here."

Norman smiled a little. "Today's not over." He shifted in the bed. "Don't let them hook me to any life-support machine, Gray. Promise? And my will, it's in a wooden box in my closet."

"Okay, Dad," Gray agreed just to soothe him. "Just rest."

Gray looked up as a beanpole of a man in green surgical scrubs walked into the room. He had a clipboard in his hands and a very serious look on his face. "I'm Dr. Gabriel York. I'm a cardiologist. Your father has had a heart attack, and we need to perform an angioplasty in order to open one of the arteries in his heart."

Gray swallowed, taking in the information. More doctors entered the room—a female anesthesiologist and another doctor who introduced himself as the ER admitting doctor. They gathered information from Gray as yet another person entered the room and thrust some papers into his dad's hand to sign. Before Gray could truly take in what was happening, they whisked his dad off to the operating room. After they left, Gray stared at the empty space where his father had been and prayed.

∂∞

Jamie looked up as Gray walked into the waiting room. His face looked ill with worry. She tried to smile reassuringly as he picked his way across the room, but her lips trembled. "Is he okay?"

"They've taken him to surgery," Gray explained. "We need to go to the fourth floor."

On the way, Gray explained in a tight voice that his father was having a heart attack and the doctors were performing an angioplasty in order to prevent further damage to his heart. Although Gray said this operation was very common, it sounded serious, and Jamie had to fight to keep the fear from showing on her face.

The surgical waiting room was empty. She and Gray dropped onto side-by-side chairs. She curled her fingers around his. "He's a strong man, Gray. He'll pull through this."

Gray nodded and gripped her hand a little tighter. He stared for a little while at the TV monitor, which was turned to CNN but had no sound. After a short time he bowed his head and closed his eyes. She realized he must be praying.

She thought about it and then closed her eyes. *Lord, there's this man, Norman Westler, and he's in surgery right now, and he needs Your help. Please don't let him die. Let him get better. Gray needs You, too, God. His hand's like ice.*

It seemed like forever, but then a tall, painfully thin man in surgical scrubs popped out from behind a closed door and marched toward them in long, unhurried strides. Jamie struggled to read his face.

"It went very well," the doctor said, holding out a cloudy-looking X-ray. "We were able to restore blood flow, but we'll have to run some more tests before we understand the extent of the damage." He pointed to the lower right chamber of the heart. "See this discolored area? It's deterioration. I suspect your father has been experiencing symptoms for some time now."

Gray frowned at the X-ray. "So you're saying this is not a new problem."

"No. Has your dad been complaining of shortness of breath, chest pain, pain in his arms, or dizziness?"

"I don't think so," Gray said. At the same time Jamie said, "Yes."

She glanced at Gray's surprised face and turned back to the doctor. "I saw him one night get dizzy. It went away after he rested."

Gray's eyes narrowed. "When was this?"

"A few days ago. The night we played Monopoly."

"Did he complain of chest pain or nausea?" the doctor asked.

"He said his stomach was a little upset. He didn't eat much dinner. Remember, Gray?"

Gray shook his head. "No. He's seemed perfectly fine to me."

"The key to surviving a heart attack is getting the proper treatment as soon as possible," the doctor said gravely. "Restoring the blood flow is critical."

Gray had a lot of questions. Jamie began writing things down for him on a scrap of paper so he could go over it later. It all seemed complicated—just the terminology was confusing—and after the doctor drew several diagrams, it became clear the doctor was trying to tell them he feared Norman was in the early stages of heart failure.

"Will he need a heart transplant?" Jamie asked and saw her own fear mirrored in Gray's eyes.

"It's too soon to tell," the doctor said.

When Norman woke up, a surgical nurse brought Gray back to the recovery area to see him, and several hours later he was taken to a room. Jamie was frightened by the bluish tint to his lips and fingernails and the paleness of his skin. Monitors flashing unfathomable information flanked him. He had an IV dripping into his arm and an oxygen tube fastened under his nose. His eyes were closed, but when Jamie squeezed his hand, she felt him grasp her fingers a little harder. She bent low so she could whisper for his ear alone. "I love you, Norman."

She and Gray didn't speak much on the way back to the house. Gray drove. His gaze, fixed on the road, discouraged conversation, and Jamie felt a lump of guilt settle directly on her vocal cords. She should have mentioned the dizzy spell to Gray. And if this wasn't enough, she feared her reckless trip down the ski hill had triggered Norman's heart attack. When she tried to apologize to Gray, he cut her off, claiming his dad's condition was not her fault.

Halle and Ivy raced out to greet them the minute Gray parked the Jeep in front of the house. Gray barely got out of the car before Halle launched herself into his arms and buried her head in his shoulder. "Shhh," Gray said in a low, soothing voice. "Grandpa is okay. He's resting now."

Ivy's eyes were large and luminous beneath the porch lights. "What's wrong with him, Mom?" she asked. "Is Mr. Westler going to be okay?"

"I think so," Jamie replied. Glancing over the top of Ivy's head, she watched Gray stroke the back of Halle's head and saw Halle's back shake with sobs.

"Grandpa had a heart attack," Gray said gently, "and he has to stay in the hospital for a few days for some tests."

Jamie put her arm across the top of Ivy's shoulders. "Come on, let's go inside. Did you and Halle get something to eat?"

"No," Ivy said. "We weren't hungry." She stared at Halle and Gray for a long moment, and it occurred to Jamie that their grief was foreign to her daughter. Ivy had never been close to anyone they'd known who'd died or had faced a life-threatening illness. She had no idea how scary and painful it could be. Jamie studied her daughter's eyes a little more closely and realized she had it all wrong. Just because Ivy had never known her father or grandparents didn't mean she was incapable of mourning their loss.

# twenty-two

Norman grew stronger, but as the doctor had suspected, there was irreversible damage to the heart. It was not immediately life threatening or bad enough to put him on the list for a heart transplant, but it was life-changing. For the rest of his life, he would have to remain on a very strict diet and exercise plan and take medications—"Horse pills," Norman called them.

On Sunday afternoon, Jamie drove Ivy back to Miss Porter's school in old Sally. When they reached Ivy's dormitory, Jamie turned off the engine. Over the knocks and rattles of the old car, she hugged her daughter. "I love you," she said.

Ivy murmured something like, "You, too." She drew back. "You're not going to forget about me meeting my grandparents, are you?"

"Of course not," Jamie promised. "When things settle down a bit, I'll call them."

Ivy started to open the car door and then stopped. "You're not going to call them, are you? There's always going to be some reason why you can't."

Jamie reminded herself to be patient, although a part of her felt a little irritated with Ivy. The last two days had been rough, and she was tired. "Of course I'm going to call them. You have to trust me, Ivy."

"When?" Ivy pressed. "When will you call them?"

Jamie bit her tongue before she spoke. "Soon." She held her hand to ward off Ivy's next question. "It depends on how Norman and Gray are doing."

Ivy shook her head rapidly back and forth. "My real grandpa could have a heart attack, just like Mr. Westler, and he could die. I wouldn't even get to know him." She wrenched open the car door. "Maybe he's already dead."

"Look," Jamie said flatly. "You know what my parents did—I would think you would have a little loyalty to me." She saw the look of disgust on Ivy's face just before her daughter slammed the door shut.

Jamie marched to the back of the car. She hauled out Ivy's suitcase and ski bag. She set these on the sidewalk and freed Ivy's skis from the rack atop the car. "When you're up in your room cataloging all the things I've done wrong, just remember that I was the one who stuck around. I was the one who loved you—who still loves you."

"I'm sorry," Ivy said. "I know. . . . It's just. . ."

Jamie put her arms around Ivy. "Hard," she finished. "But we'll figure this out together."

Ivy wriggled out from Jamie's arms. "Are you mad at me?"

"No. Are you mad at me?"

"No," Ivy said. "But you'll call this week, right?"

Jamie sighed. Ivy had no idea how much work was waiting for Jamie back at the office or what she was asking Jamie to do. "Ivy, please," she said, then relented. "I'll try." She started to roll Ivy's suitcase toward the house, but Ivy's hand on her arm stopped her. "It's okay, Mom. I've got it."

"You've got the skis and ski bag." Jamie took another step toward the building.

"Mom!" Ivy said sharply. When Jamie turned around, she added, "I can do both. You ought to get going." Then she whispered, "Old Sally is leaking oil on the road. It's embarrassing."

Jamie hurried back to the car just as a white Infiniti pulled to the curb. A well-groomed woman stepped out. For a moment their eyes met. Jamie watched the gaze of the other woman slide away from her, the way someone might glance away from a homeless person.

Jamie slammed the old Buick's door. Turning the key, she punched the gas. "Make Norman proud," she said. The Buick backfired as if it were expelling a cannonball, and a large black cloud blocked the view out the rear window. Jamie started to laugh as she roared away from the curb.

❧

They brought Norman home on Monday. Gray wanted to take his dad straight to the house, but Norman insisted on going to the ski lodge. He intended to get back to work in the rental shop, but Gray put his foot down. They began to argue, but Jamie stepped in and negotiated a compromise. They would take Norman to the ski hill, but only if he agreed to settle in a comfortable chair in front of the lodge windows.

"You want some tea?" Jamie asked as she pulled a woolen throw higher on Norman's lap. "A piece of fruit?"

"I want a chili dog," Norman stated. At the look on her face, he added, "I'm joking. The two of you get going." He pointed a knobby finger at Gray. "You've got lessons to teach and a hill to run. And you,"—he pointed to Jamie—"I want to see you coming down Alice's Alley, hopefully slower than the last time I saw you."

Jamie felt herself cringe, although Norman had assured her that she hadn't caused his heart attack.

"I'm teasing," Norman said. "The two of you have to stop wearing funeral faces. Shoo. Get going."

Gray said, "I don't have any lessons scheduled today. Besides, Dad, I'd really like to hang out with you."

"Don't take this wrong," Norman growled, "but I'd rather be alone. I just want to sit here with the sun on my face and nobody telling me what to do—or trying to stick another needle into me."

"Dad," Gray said gently. "You just got home. At least let one of us stay until you get settled." Gray glanced at Jamie, who nodded in agreement.

"No," Norman thundered and turned an alarming shade of red. "I'd rather ski myself off a cliff than be treated as an invalid."

"Gray," Jamie said, laying her hand on his tense arm. "Maybe we better do what he says."

"She's right," Norman said. "Besides, the best medicine would be knowing the two of you are on the hill having fun. Alice and I made some great memories on that hill. You two should, too." He winked at Gray.

After Gray asked Doreen Mosley, who was working in the concession stand, to keep an eye on his dad, he and Jamie headed to the locker rooms to change. She worried about leaving Norman alone, but thought it would be okay if it was only for a short time. She understood, too, that Norman needed to exert his independence.

She met Gray at the double chairlift. The line wasn't long, and soon the two of them were treetop level and climbing higher. After spending so much time at the hospital, the air smelled incredibly fresh and healthy to them. The heat of the sun contrasted with the freezing temperatures, and the bulk of Gray seated on the bench beside her warmed something deep inside.

"He's arguing and being bossy," Gray said. "I think that's a good sign."

"Yeah," Jamie agreed. "But maybe after this run, we should check on him."

Gray nodded. "Good idea." He glanced at her. "I haven't thanked you enough for all you've done for us, Jamie. I don't know how I would have gotten through the last week without you."

"I'm glad I was here," Jamie replied. "And I wouldn't have been here if you hadn't taken in me and Ivy. You're a good man, Gray."

They rode in silence and then, very casually as if he were only stretching, Gray laid his arm over the back of the bench seat. Jamie's heart started to beat a little faster. Equally casually, as if she were merely shifting into a more comfortable position, she leaned into the curve of his arm.

Neither said anything, but Jamie wondered if his heart was

beating as fast as hers. She could hardly breathe, and all she could think about was how good it felt to sit so close to him, how strong his body felt and how perfectly she fit into the crook of his arm.

She lifted her face and found him looking down at her, a soft, searching expression in his brown eyes. She didn't resist when he bent his head and kissed her. It was over in a flash, but Jamie saw something serious in his eyes as he pulled away from her.

"You don't know how long I've wanted to do that," he said.

The wind shook the lift lightly. Jamie felt the chill right through her parka. "Gray," she said. "I like you a lot, but tomorrow. . .I'm going back to Greenwich. My job," she said. "I can't take any more time off."

This was true, but it was only part of the reason. They rolled over another support tower, and the top of the mountain came into view. The snow-covered ground and trees braced against the wind seemed to mirror something lonely and empty in her heart.

"Greenwich and Woodbury are just a little over an hour apart. I'd really like to see you again."

"Me, too, but. . ." Jamie struggled to put something in words that she really didn't fully understand herself. "I need to figure some things out first. Alone." She said the last word gently, but watched Gray's features tighten.

The lift reached the top of the mountain, and Jamie skied off the chair next to Gray. Although they moved out of the way of the lift line, it was unnecessary. The hilltop was empty. A cold wind whipped across the peak, stinging her cheeks. Jamie's nose started to run, and she wiped it with a tissue, thinking she must look awful. *Talk to him,* something said. She wanted to ignore the voice—did Gray really need to hear the awful story? Yet she sensed it would be a mistake to ignore such a strong feeling.

"When I was growing up," she began, "I was the girl who got

straight As, made varsity cheerleader, and played Mary in the church's Nativity play, but all I wanted was my parents to see me—not my achievements. I wanted them to love me unconditionally. At the same time, I was afraid not to be the daughter they wanted.

"There was this boy on the football team—Devon Brown. He held the high school record for scoring touchdowns. He was also a rebel—the kind of kid who talked back to teachers when they deserved it and wore his hair twice as long as he was supposed to." She glanced up at Gray's eyes to see if he'd figured out where this whole story was going and if his opinion of her already was changing. "I wanted to be like him. I didn't want to care what the world thought about me. I thought I could be a different person with him.

"So I pursued him," Jamie continued. "At every game I cheered louder than anybody else for him. I decorated his locker and made up personal holidays in his name. I wore the clothes I thought he'd like and flirted until he noticed me. We started going out, and just like I hoped, I began feeling a bit like a rebel."

She was getting to the part of the story she dreaded most. "One night Devon asked if I wanted to drive to the beach. I knew from the way he said it and the look in his eye that it was going to be more than that. I thought it would be the final piece of finding myself."

She could almost hear the sound of Devon's car door slamming shut behind her, and the rumble of the motor as they drove away from her parents' house. They'd parked in a lonely spot where they could see the black water of the Atlantic rippling in the moonlight. She'd felt fear, cold as the hand Devon placed on her neck, wash over her. *I love you, baby,* he'd said.

"Devon didn't want to be a father, and my parents didn't want to be grandparents, so they sent me to live with Aunt Bea in Maine. They said I was beyond their help and should beg for God's forgiveness." She looked Gray straight in the eye. "I've loved Ivy since before she was born. How was I supposed to tell God that I wish I hadn't gotten into that car with Devon Brown? If I hadn't done that, I wouldn't have her."

Gray's eyes held the kindest expression she had ever seen. "There are no accidental children—they're all designed by the Lord. I don't think God would want the circumstances of Ivy's birth to keep you from having a relationship with Him. He doesn't focus on sin."

"I can't ask for His forgiveness," Jamie said sadly, "because I'm not sorry for what I did. If I didn't get in that car, I wouldn't have Ivy. Don't you see?"

"I think if you spent time with the Lord and got to know Him more deeply, you would think differently. God loves you unconditionally," Gray said. "He wants no walls between you. I don't think you do, either."

Many times in Jamie's life she'd felt herself reaching out for God, then jerking her hand back. Wanting His love but fearing she didn't deserve it. She flexed her cold fingers and shifted her weight against the top of her boots. This was all true, but if she were honest—truly honest with herself—she'd admit it wasn't just fear of rejection that kept her from God. Part of her hadn't wanted to give up control of her life to anyone. She'd wanted her parents and the whole world to see that Jamie King could make it on her own. What she saw now, however, was how foolish she'd been.

She looked at Gray, at the gentleness in his dark eyes and the tousled brown hair framing his suntanned face. He'd lost his wife, almost his father, and a bad year of weather could cripple him financially. Yet there was an inner core of strength about him. She remembered the expression on his face as he'd sat beside his father's hospital bed praying, and she felt something inside her start to give.

"Jamie," Gray prompted gently. "What are you thinking?"

*About you,* she thought. *About what it must feel like to have such a strong faith and how I'm scared that I'll never be like that.* "We should get going," she said at last. "Norman needs you, and I have to start packing. I'm leaving tomorrow, remember?"

He tugged gently on her scarf. "Yes, but you don't have to. You could stay and run the B & B. Mrs. Dodges could help my dad in the ski shop."

Jamie understood he wasn't just talking about a job. He was talking about them. Their future. Her heart started to race. She stared at his lips, wondering what it might be like to kiss him and knowing instinctively that it would be overwhelming. She could feel parts of herself dissolving just thinking about it. It was tempting, but there wasn't just herself to consider.

"Thanks, Gray," she managed to reply, "but I wouldn't be able to keep Ivy in private school. She deserves a chance to get the best education I can give her."

"Maybe you deserve something, too," Gray said. "A chance to be happy. Maybe it's time you stopped punishing yourself for something that happened a long time ago. I understand if you want to go back to Greenwich, but it doesn't mean what we started here has to end."

It made perfect sense, and it wasn't as if she didn't want the same thing, too. The longing for him to put his arms around her was an ache so strong it was nearly unbearable. At the same time, she cringed at the thought of him seeing the apartment she couldn't afford and learning about her maxed-out credit cards. He deserved better than the messed-up life she had to offer.

She could change, though. Straighten out her life. All she needed was a little more time. One good sale could turn everything around. Two sales and she'd be debt free. The market really heated up in the spring, and by then she might have other things figured out, too—like Ivy's obsession with meeting Jamie's parents.

For his own sake, she needed to make Gray understand she wasn't saying no—just not now. She took a deep breath of icy air and began to speak. It was hard, but not impossible, to move past the look of hurt and disappointment that formed in Gray's dark brown eyes.

# twenty-three

Her apartment felt cold and empty. Jamie kicked off her Ferragamos at the door and pulled her suitcase through the plush white carpeting. She turned up the heat, but continued to wander about her apartment, touching things, trying to feel a sense of homecoming.

She changed into a dark gray pantsuit and spent forty-five minutes fussing with her hair and makeup. When she got into old Sally, she had every intention of going straight to work. However, she surprised herself by driving right past the office building.

She had a vague idea of going to Todd's Point to walk the beach or picking up some groceries at the A & P, but when she spotted the mottled gray stones of an old Methodist church, the car seemed to turn into the parking lot of its own accord.

The church was empty, and she settled herself into a hard-backed pew. The light through the stained glass illuminated an image of Jesus on the cross. She thought about Him, about how much He had suffered and yet how much He loved. She remembered all the prayers of her youth—*make me a cheerleader, make me blonder, thinner. Make Devon love me.* When had she ever closed her eyes and given herself to Him? Putting her face in her hands, she let the tears fall.

She wasn't sure how long she sat there, but when she looked up a man in blue jeans and a shirt with a black collar was standing next to her. He had deep-set blue eyes and a wreath of gray hair around a shiny bald scalp. Jamie wiped her eyes self-consciously. "I'm sorry," she said.

"It's all right."

His voice was deep and comforting. Jamie felt as if she could tell him anything and his eyes would still shine with the same deep kindness. "I've made a mess of things," she said. "I need to change."

He nodded sympathetically. "You've come to the right place," he said.

&

The stately brick colonial had not changed in the years since Jamie had last seen it. The azalea bushes grew the same height along the front of the house; the shutters gleamed the same glossy black; and the same winter mix of holly, juniper, and ivy grew in the oversized concrete planters flanking the brick walkway.

Jamie's fingers trembled as they hovered above the doorbell. She bit her lower lip and reminded herself that she wasn't seventeen anymore.

The long slow chimes drifted softly through the double doors. *Stop it heart,* she ordered. *Stop racing. It's distracting.* A moment later the door opened. Her father's lanky frame filled the wedge of space. One glance at his powder blue cashmere sweater and pressed wool slacks and Jamie felt swept back in time. She tried to smile and failed. "Hello, Dad."

"Jamie," he said quietly. "Come in."

She recognized the Chippendale table in the foyer. The glossy black-framed mirror hanging over it was new, as was the trendy zebra-print fabric on the old camelback sofa in the living room.

"Let's go in my office." Her dad gestured to the room immediately to their right.

"Is Mom home?" She winced at the hopeful note in her voice.

"No."

Jamie kept her back straight as she followed her dad into his office. She settled herself into a hunter green leather chair. Her father took a seat behind a glossy, key-holed desk and pulled out a yellow legal pad as if he intended to take notes on their meeting.

She moistened her dry lips. "Dad," she said, "I'm here to ask a favor."

He nodded as if he had expected no less. "How much?" Before she even replied, the drawer to his desk opened, and he pulled out a checkbook.

His words stung—as they'd been meant to. "I'm not here for money." She clenched the strap of her purse. "I'm here for Ivy, your granddaughter, remember?"

"I remember," her father echoed quietly.

Jamie pulled out Ivy's most recent school portrait and laid it on her father's desk. "She wants to meet you and Mom."

Her dad removed his glasses, studied the lenses for spots, and then replaced them. Only after this agonizingly slow process did he pick up the photo. "So this is the child."

Her father's face could have been made of granite for all the emotion he displayed. He had aged, though. Jamie saw it in the deepening grooves in his face and the receding line of his silver hair. "She has his coloring," he said without looking up. "But your features."

"Ivy's a straight-A student at Miss Porter's School. Her debate team went to state last year, and she just won her age category in an interclub ski race." There were other things she could tell him—the way Ivy's eyes lit up when she laughed, the sweetness of her voice when she sang in the shower, how her nose curled in a cute way when she stuck her toes in cold pool water.

"Miss Porter's, you say?"

"This is her first year."

"Ed Nickelson has a granddaughter going there. Shelly. You know her?"

Jamie shook her head. Truth was, she barely knew Ivy's friends.

"It's an expensive school," her father said. "You must be doing well to send her there."

"I'm a realtor," she said. The rest wasn't any of his business.

"So what do you think? Do you want to meet her?" She held her breath, hoping he would and terrified for the same reason.

"I'll have to talk about this with your mother." He seemed to hesitate and then added, "You look good, Jamie."

How could he hesitate? How could he not jump on this opportunity? Here she was, offering him the most precious gift he could ever receive and all he could say was she looked good? Jamie felt her temper rise. Why was she so surprised? At the heart of things, he was a selfish person—a man with a moral code so rigid he could not bring himself to forgive his only child.

She curled the strap of her purse tightly. "One thing, Dad. If you decide to meet her, I want to be very clear that you will do nothing, say nothing that could in any way hurt Ivy more than you have already."

His face remained impassive. "Hurt her? At the time, Jamie, your mother and I did what we thought was best for you and the baby." His face softened. "You couldn't stay here—people would have made your life miserable. And the child, she would have been labeled."

Jamie felt the blood rush to her face. "You think being disowned was so much better?" She shook her head. "You weren't afraid for me or Ivy—you were afraid for yourselves. We would have been an embarrassment to you."

He took off his glasses and raked his hands through the thin strands of his silver hair. "I won't deny that we thought about that. It wasn't the deciding factor, though. We felt if you realized how hard it would be to be a single parent, you'd give the baby up for adoption. We thought the child would be better off with an older, married couple."

"You were wrong," Jamie said, rising to her feet.

Her father's gaze was steady, but she saw a sheen of perspiration on his forehead. "Don't think it's been easy for us, either. Don't think we haven't suffered because of what we did."

Jamie set her business card on the desk. "I'm sorry for that, and I'm sorry that Ivy wants to meet you, but here we are." She looked around at the stacks of legal books on the dark wood of the built-in shelves and knew her father saw things in black or white, right or wrong. "Call me when you and Mom make a decision."

She was too upset to drive straight home. Instead she headed for the Methodist church. The choir was singing when she walked into the chapel. She slipped into a pew and bowed her head, thinking some hurts were too deep to be healed and feeling like she'd failed. She dreaded telling Ivy about the meeting. After a few moments, the reverend joined her on the bench. He sat quietly next to her, studied her face, and asked, "How'd it go?"

Jamie shrugged. "Okay, I guess. He said he'd have to think about it."

He nodded. "Let me pray for you."

"Thank you," she said. Joining hands with the minister, she looked steadily into his eyes. It took a moment to work the words past the lump in her throat. "I feel so broken," she admitted. "Everything hurts."

His grip tightened. "You're not alone."

❧

Her cell phone rang on her way home. When she saw the Connecticut number, her heart began to race, and she pulled over to the side of the road. "Jamie King," she answered crisply.

"It's your father," her dad said.

She felt her muscles go rigid. A terrible fear crept along her spine. She couldn't bear it if he disappointed Ivy.

"You left your gloves," he said.

"Oh." Her heart sank. He could keep the gloves.

"You can come pick them up on Sunday," her father said. "If you like, you could stay for lunch. And bring the girl—Ivy—if she can get away from school."

"I'll check with her," Jamie replied calmly as if her heart wasn't firmly lodged in her throat and every muscle hadn't gone limp. "But it'll probably be fine. Would you like us to bring something?"

There was a long pause and then her father said, "No, just yourselves." His voice gave nothing away, and he quickly hung up. Afterward Jamie stared at her cell phone and realized they had not set a time. She pictured her dad sitting at his desk realizing the same thing and trying to decide what to do about it. She wondered if his hands were shaking as hard as hers right now.

# twenty-four

"Where'd you hide my car keys, Gray?" Norman asked. "I want to take Sally for a spin."

Gray had come into the ski shop on the pretext of needing a wrench to fix one of the mountain bikes. It was April and soon people would be coming to Pilgrim's Peak to bike the ski trails. Mostly, though, he wanted to check on his father. "I've got some free time. Where do you want to go?"

His dad's brows pushed together. "Stop treating me like an invalid, checking up on me every two minutes."

Gray grinned. "It's been two hours since I saw you at breakfast. Besides, I need a sprocket wrench."

Norman retrieved the tool from a drawer. "I want to drive. I have a clean bill of health from the doctor. I'm even legal, remember?"

How could Gray forget the trip to the motor vehicles department? While waiting in line, his dad had flirted with a woman with a swooping eagle tattooed to her shoulder, and the minute Norman found out she liked bikes, he'd invited her to Pilgrim's Peak. Fortunately for Gray, it turned out she liked motorcycles and not mountain bikes, and she had turned him down.

"I know you want to drive," Gray said, "but I haven't put any oil in Sally recently, and I don't think we have any in the garage."

In truth, he was afraid to go anywhere near the car. When Jamie had returned it several weeks ago, it'd held the very faintest trace of her perfume. He'd sat in the Buick like a lovesick teenager, breathing her in and wondering if she ever intended to come back.

"I'm sure there's enough oil to get me to a gas station." Norman picked up a file and began rubbing the tool against the edge of a ski. Even though it would be months before anyone rented skis, he liked to spend the off-season getting the equipment in perfect condition. "I don't know how much time I've got," he stated flatly.

"According to the doctor, if you stay away from the chili dogs and doughnuts, you'll be here for years." Gray studied the plank floors worn into the color of dirt by hundreds, maybe thousands of ski boots clumping across them. "If you want to drive somewhere, at least let me come with you."

His dad snorted. "You'll only slow me down."

Gray laughed. "What are you talking about?"

His father's face looked thinner, and there were lingering shadows beneath his eyes that hadn't gone away since his heart attack. "The only thing I really care about is you, Gray, and Halle. I'm not going to be here forever you know."

Not another death speech. Gray willed himself to listen patiently.

"Before I die, I want to make sure you'll be happy."

"Dad," Gray interrupted, despite himself. "Halle and I are fine. And you're going to be here for a long, long time."

His dad banged the file onto the worktable. "And when Halle goes off to college, what are you going to do, Gray? Rattle around this ski hill like a ghost? Now give me my car keys and let me get to work."

"Work, Dad?"

"Finding you a wife. We made good progress with Jamie— and to be honest, I was a little disappointed on how that turned out—but since she doesn't seem to be the right one for you, we have to keep looking."

Gray flinched. The mention of Jamie's name could do that to him. Then his brain registered the last part of the sentence. "Dad, I don't need you to find me a wife."

"Obviously you do. Now, Gray, you didn't like the women at Talbots, the beauty salon, or the movie theater. I'm thinking of taking Boomer to the new dog-grooming place in Southbury. I'll stake out the waiting room and call if I see someone promising."

His dad was joking. Gray rubbed his eyes. When his father's face came back into focus, Gray saw the same look of concern in his dad's brown eyes. "You're serious," he said.

"Of course. Usually women who like animals are caring people. I don't know why I didn't think of this sooner."

It was all starting to make horrifying sense now. "Dad, tell me all those so-called car accidents weren't attempts to set me up with women?"

"How else was I going to delay the girls long enough for you to see them?"

"You could have hurt someone." Gray raked his hands through his hair. "Not to mention you inconvenienced everyone, damaged a lot of cars, and nearly gave me a heart attack every time you called and said you'd been in an accident." Gray studied his dad's stoic features. "You're not even sorry you made a mess of things."

"Love is messy," his dad stated gravely. "Get over it, Gray. Now tell me where you hid the keys."

Gray shook his head. If he had to, he'd bury those keys in the backyard. "Not until I'm sure you aren't going to drive into some poor woman's car."

"I will when you stop waiting for love to show up on your front doorstep." His father's gravelly voice sharpened. "Because it looks like God tried that once—and I don't think He's going to do it again."

Gray's face burned. He clenched his jaw to keep from saying something he'd regret later. Turning, he stormed out of the room, his work boots echoing in the empty building. His dad thought he knew everything, but he knew nothing. Nothing at all.

Gray shoved the door to the ski lodge open and stepped into the strong April sun. He'd given Jamie months, and she still hadn't called. The cloudless blue sky taunted him, and he kicked a rock that had the nerve to get in his way. He glanced at the near-empty parking lot. His dad was right about one thing—he highly doubted Jamie King was going to show up on his doorstep again.

His gaze remained on his Jeep. Nope. Jamie King might not show up on his doorstep, but there was nothing keeping him from showing up on hers.

It didn't take long to find her address—he wasn't without computer skills. By late afternoon, he found himself in the parking lot of a high-rise apartment building in Old Greenwich. There was a Hertz moving truck parked in the front. His stomach clenched at the sight of Jamie standing beside it.

She was standing next to a powerfully built man with dark hair and olive-colored skin. The guy said something that made Jamie laugh. Something about the guy seemed familiar. Gray clenched his fists as the brawny guy gave Jamie a kiss on the cheek.

"That ought to do it," Brawny Guy said. "We'll see you at the new place."

"Thanks, Devon," Jamie said.

Gray's heart sank as the reason Jamie hadn't called became clear to him. He felt like an idiot. Mending relationships had obviously included a renewed one with Ivy's father. He turned to leave, hoping she wouldn't see him.

❧

The shape of the back was right and so was the color of the hair, but the cut was wrong. It was much too short. She squinted her eyes. Gray?

"Gray!" The man didn't stop. She started running, caught up to him, and grabbed his arm, half expecting herself to be wrong.

Gray turned around, and the expression on his face chilled her to the bone. She released him. "Is Norman okay?"

"He and Halle are fine."

Jamie looked at him, confused. He'd cut his hair since the last time she'd seen him, and his jaw was clean-shaven. He seemed thinner, too, and his eyes were guarded. "I don't understand," she said.

He shrugged. "I came to see you, but I can tell this isn't the right time." He clicked his remote, and the locks popped open. "Good luck with the move, Jamie."

"I owe you a phone call," she admitted, studying the tense line of his mouth. "I was going to call you from my new place."

His mouth twisted. "You don't owe me anything. Look, I know you need to get going. You don't want to keep Devon waiting."

Jamie put her hand on his arm. His muscles felt as tight as steel cables. "He's just helping me move."

"You don't need to explain anything to me." Gray pulled the car door open and climbed onto the seat.

"Look," Jamie said, hauling uselessly at his arm. "I don't want you to go away thinking there's something between me and Devon when there isn't. He's just trying to make up for the past."

Gray's eyebrows lifted. "Looks like he's succeeding."

Jamie pressed closer to the car. She wanted to yank the keys out of his hands. "Gray, don't. He's Ivy's father, and that's it."

"He kissed you," Gray said flatly.

"Devon kisses everyone—that's just him." Jamie looked in his eyes and wondered how to make him believe her. "Gray, he's only in my life again because of Ivy. She needs to know him. I'm not interested in him or anyone else." She paused and registered the disbelieving twist of his lips. "I'm only interested in you."

The air went very still around them. "Then why haven't you called me? Why did you drop off Sally without even seeing me?"

To her dismay, Jamie's throat started to tighten. "I couldn't."

"Why not?"

She bit her lower lip. "Because I was afraid if I saw you or talked to you, I wouldn't be able to stay away from you. I told you, when I came to you, I wanted things to be as perfect as I could make them."

He looked at her for a long time, then the seat creaked as he stepped out of the driver's seat. He folded his arms and gazed sternly down at her. "You have to stop thinking everything has to be perfect," Gray said. "Because it's never going to happen. There's always going to be some problem, some obstacle that gets in the way, and that's called life. People who love each other should go through these things together."

"I'm not talking about a clogged sink," Jamie said, afraid to focus on his last sentence. "I'm talking about financial debt. I'm talking about a daughter who is very confused about who she is."

"You have some challenges," Gray agreed. "But if you didn't have them, I never would have met you."

She told him about the beautiful old church she had accidentally found and the reverend who had talked her into coming back for Sunday service. The message had been about forgiveness, and Jamie had cried when she realized how much she was hurting herself and Ivy by not forgiving the people who had hurt her.

"I'm coming to see that I was wrong about a lot of things, Gray. Most of all for not trusting God. I didn't think He could forgive me, much less love me. I'm still trying to wrap my mind around that concept." She shook her head. "All these years I stayed away from Him, but He was still watching out for me. How could I not see that?"

"You see it now."

"I have a long way to go and so much to learn."

"We all do. But we don't have to go through things alone."

Jamie shook her head. They were starting to talk in circles. "Sometimes you do."

"Does that mean I have to have everything in my life in perfect order before you could love me? Does Halle have to be able to play a perfect set of scales on the french horn, or does my dad have to pass his next physical?"

"Of course not." Jamie was horrified to think he might believe that.

"And you don't, either." Gray lifted her fingers and kissed them gently. "I've missed you, Jamie, and I don't want to miss another day without you in it. I wake up thinking about you, and all day I wonder what you're doing. I go to bed thinking about you. I want to start a life with you today. Right here. Right now."

She searched her heart for answers. The truth was, she didn't want to turn Gray away. It didn't mean she'd stop struggling to change her life or get sidetracked in her desire to build a relationship with God. Learning about the Lord was going to be a lifelong journey—a journey she wanted to take with Gray at her side. "If you really mean that," Jamie said, "then I could really use your help moving my couch into my new place." She started to tell him about the great view of the Mianus River and then said, "It's a basement apartment and much cheaper. I'm on a budget now."

"I'll help you move—today and when you're ready to come back to Pilgrim's Peak."

Jamie started to smile. "You sure you aren't just wanting my lemon blueberry muffins?"

"No," Gray said gravely. "I like the lemon cheesecake ones with the crumble topping much better."

"As long as we're clear," Jamie said, savoring the expression in his eyes, which she knew had nothing to do with muffins. "And if I were to agree to start seeing you again, would the arrangement include private ski lessons?"

"As many as you want."

"In that case," Jamie said, smiling, "I think I might want a lifetime of them."

Gray's eyes crinkled. He smiled as he tilted his head toward her. "I think that could be arranged."

# twenty-five

Jamie lifted her veil over the back of the seat. Beside her, Ivy pulled down the safety bar as the chairlift swept them into the crisp February afternoon. The white gossamer fabric streamed behind them like a flag as they started up the mountain. A white parka and ski pants weren't exactly the wedding outfit Jamie had once imagined herself wearing, but it felt right. Better than right, actually. Perfect.

"You nervous, Mom?"

"A little," Jamie admitted. "Don't ski too close to me after the ceremony. I might run into you by accident."

Ivy made a face. "You're not going to run into anyone, Mom."

She'd only been joking, but Ivy had missed it completely. Jamie studied her daughter's lovely profile. "What? What aren't you telling me?"

"It's stupid." Ivy sighed.

"Please, Ivy. Tell me. I want this to be a happy day." She twisted to see Ivy's face better. "You are happy, aren't you?"

"Of course." Ivy studied the tips of her skis. "But I still don't know what to call them—the Mr. Westlers."

"I thought you were going to call Gray, 'Dad,' and Norman, 'Grandpa.'"

Ivy waggled her skis. "I know, but I've been thinking, it's going to be confusing having multiple dads and grandpas."

Jamie smiled and patted Ivy's leg. "It's a good problem to have, isn't it?"

"But it's weird, too, to think of you moving to Woodbury and living at Pilgrim's Peak."

"I know," Jamie said, holding her veil as a strong wind rocked the chairlift in the same spot it always did. "But I'll be closer to Farmington, and it'll be easier to see you." She grinned. "If you want me to, that is."

Two bright spots of color appeared in Ivy's pale face. Her face morphed into a series of expressions before her lips formed any words at all. "Well, I'm kinda thinking I might not want to stay at Miss Porter's. I'm kinda thinking I might want to train with Mr. Grayson and start going to some more ski races. It would be easier to do that if I lived with you," Ivy said.

"You could do that," Jamie said eagerly. "I'd love for you to do that."

"I'm not quite sure," Ivy said. "I don't think Woodbury is going to have teachers as good as Miss Porter's, and I don't want to leave my friends. I really want to go to a good college, maybe Yale or Princeton."

"Woodbury High is a great school," Jamie said. "You could go there and still get into a good school."

"I don't know," Ivy said. "Part of me wants to stay at Miss Porter's and. . ."

"What?" Jamie asked. To her dismay, she saw Ivy's lips tremble and her eyes fill with tears.

"Part of me wants to stay here. I'm kinda scared you're going to forget about me if I don't."

"Oh honey," Jamie said, hugging her as much as the narrow seat would allow. "I could never forget about you—I love you so much. I always have, and I always will. Nothing can change that. Nothing."

"You'll have Gray and Halle. You'll be a family without me, and you'll have all these inside jokes I won't understand."

"Ivy," Jamie said. "Nobody in the world could ever replace you or make me love you less. Do you love me less because you're starting to get to know your father and your grandparents?"

Ivy shook her head. "No, but they aren't coming to live with us."

They never really went away, did they? The old hurts and deep fears. They popped up like moles in that silly arcade game. As soon as you bopped one on the head, another mole popped up in another place. She linked her arm through Ivy's and wiggled closer on the bench seat.

"If you want to want to change your mind and go to Woodbury, you're welcome to do it. You know I would love it."

"But then Grandma and Grandpa King will be disappointed, and they've offered to pay half of my tuition. I should stay at Miss Porter's."

Jamie patted her daughter's leg. "Helping you financially is their way of saying they love you. You should do what you think will make you the happiest." She paused as a skier passing beneath them stopped to shout his congratulations. "Let's both pray about it. I haven't always asked for the Lord's guidance, and I've made a lot of mistakes because of that."

Ivy pointed to the glittering diamond in her ear. "I love you, Mom. When we get off the lift, I want to give you the diamonds as a wedding gift—they're the best thing I have to give you."

"You're the best gift," Jamie said and started to cry. When they reached the top of the mountain, Ivy practically had to haul her out of the lift seat and down the ramp. Ivy solemnly wiped her cheeks with a tissue and then threaded the studs through Jamie's earlobes. "You're perfect now," Ivy declared.

Gray waited at the top of Alice's Alley next to Reverend Blaymires. Halle stood at his side, next to Norman, who had driven to the top of the mountain in the Sno-Cat. Nearby, a group of the Westlers' closest friends hovered nearby, ready to witness the ceremony and then ski down the hill with them. Jamie waved at Jaya and Misty who had driven up from Greenwich. Standing beside them looking very out of place were Jamie's parents. Her mother's feet had to be freezing in her stylish but impractical leather boots. She smiled, though, when she saw Jamie. Her father gave her a curt nod. She supposed this was supposed to mean approval but she wasn't quite sure. It was hard to tell with her parents, but their presence was another step forward in their relationship.

Jamie's gaze returned to Gray and stayed there. Framed by the immense blue sky, it almost looked as if he waited for her on the edge of the world. Of course this wasn't true—she'd skied this trail enough to know that even though the trail couldn't be seen until you skied right up to it, it was there. She thought faith was like that—sometimes you couldn't see very far ahead or know exactly where it was leading you, but it was always there, a never-ending path for all who cared to walk it.

Jamie squeezed Ivy's hand, gave thanks to God, and glided steadily toward her future.

# epilogue

Jamie powered up the video camera as the Woodbury Royals marching band took the field for the half-time show. She scanned the sea of blue and black uniforms for Halle's slender form. Fortunately, there were only three french horn players and the other two were tall guys.

"There she is, Gray!" Jamie zoomed in on Halle's face. "You see her?"

"Yeah, she's on the forty-yard line," Gray said calmly, but he was leaning forward on the bleachers, and his body radiated energy.

"Can't she wear a different colored plume on her hat so she's easier to see?" Norman complained. He was proudly wearing a Woodbury Royals marching band sweatshirt under his Woodbury Royals Windbreaker.

The show started with a melody led by the flutes and clarinets, then the brass and drums kicked in and the stadium resonated with the power of the full band. Jamie trained the camera on Halle, but lost her in a band-wide shuffle that sorted itself in an eyeblink into an enormous winged formation. Jamie pulled the camera back for a wider angle.

"They're great," Norman said loudly, applauding as the color guard threw bright blue and white flags into the air, catching them as the band belted out the music. "They should march at the Rose Bowl—or the White House."

Jamie's throat tightened as the band effortlessly shifted formations. She wished Ivy were there to see the show, but hoped she was having fun with Jamie's parents in Manhattan. Ivy'd be back tomorrow morning. Gray and the girls planned to go running together in order to get in shape for the coming ski season. Ivy planned to try out for the Chargers—Woodbury High's ski team. Ivy was determined to qualify for the varsity team by having the fastest time. Her daughter also planned to graduate at the top of her class—a feat the guidance counselor felt was well within Ivy's capabilities. Jamie was just glad that Ivy was happy with the transfer of schools and her new life in Woodbury.

The tempo of the music changed. In the center of the field, a lone trumpet player stepped forward. His silver instrument gleamed under the stadium lights as he pointed the instrument upward and played a flawless solo.

"And he's just a sophomore," Norman said. "That kid is amazing. He never misses a note."

The rest of the band kicked in. Jamie strained to hear the notes of the french horns. Halle, surprisingly, was developing a talent that continued to astound and thrill them all. Before Jamie knew it, the performance finished, and the band members marched proudly off the field. Turning off the camera, Jamie slipped her hand into Gray's. "That was awesome! Even better than last week."

"You say that every week," Gray pointed out, but he was smiling.

"And I mean it every week." Jamie smiled as the football team returned to the field.

They were well into the third quarter when Gray touched her arm. "Look," he said. "The kid who played the trumpet solo is climbing up on the band director's platform."

Jamie had never seen anyone but the band director on top of the ladder. The boy was very tall, thin, and blond. He had a megaphone in his hands and a determined look on his face. When he reached the top of the platform, a sudden hush fell over the entire band. "Halle Westler," the boy's voice boomed over the megaphone. "Will you go to homecoming with me?"

Gray shot her a frozen, panicked look before returning his gaze to the boy on the platform. "Did you hear that?"

Norman laughed gleefully. "It's starting," he said. "Thank God I'm here to see it."

Halle stood up and handed someone her instrument and her hat. She bounded down the bleacher steps with her long pony-tail bouncing behind her. She reached the blond boy, who had climbed down the ladder just in time to meet her. Jamie peered around the man in front of her for a better view. She watched her stepdaughter walk into the boy's arms. "I think that's a yes," she said.

"I can see that," Gray said dryly. "I don't think I'm ready for this."

"I don't think that matters," Norman said and thumped Gray's back. "I give that kid a lot of credit," he said. "Not just anyone could ask a girl out in front of everyone like that." He gave Jamie a nod. "I approve."

"Dad," Gray protested. "You don't even know the kid."

"Some things you know in your heart. Besides, Halle's been hoping for this."

"How do you know?"

"I eavesdropped. How else am I supposed to find out anything interesting?"

"Dad," Gray said. "You're awful."

Norman just laughed. "It wasn't my fault. I was napping in my chair, and when I woke up she was talking to Ivy about this boy who plays trumpet."

Jamie smiled, but most of her attention was on Halle and the blond boy. They were still standing at the base of the director's ladder. Halle's lips moved as the boy looked down, smiling. They were so young and vulnerable. She ached to hold them both in her hands and watch over them so neither of them ever hurt the other. Just for a second, she saw a glimmer of the girl she had been, standing off to the side, almost lost in the shadows, watching.

She felt her heart tug. That girl had been so lonely, so lost, and so unhappy. That girl had tried to hide her pain and be somebody she wasn't. She wished she could go back in time and tell her that everything was going to be all right. She'd put her arms around this girl and whisper the words that Jamie wished she'd understood so many years ago.

*God loves you. He loves you unconditionally, and He will never leave you.*

The girl disappeared as Halle and the boy climbed back into the stands. Gray slipped his arm across the back of Jamie's shoulders. She leaned against his side and settled back to watch the rest of the game.

# A Letter To Our Readers

Dear Reader:

In order that we might better contribute to your reading enjoyment, we would appreciate your taking a few minutes to respond to the following questions. We welcome your comments and read each form and letter we receive. When completed, please return to the following:

Fiction Editor
Heartsong Presents
PO Box 719
Uhrichsville, Ohio 44683

1. Did you enjoy reading *A Still, Small Voice* by Kim O'Brien?
   ❏ Very much! I would like to see more books by this author!
   ❏ Moderately. I would have enjoyed it more if

   _____

   _____

   _____

2. Are you a member of **Heartsong Presents**? ❏ Yes ❏ No
   If no, where did you purchase this book? _____

   _____

3. How would you rate, on a scale from 1 (poor) to 5 (superior), the cover design? _____

4. On a scale from 1 (poor) to 10 (superior), please rate the following elements.

   ____ Heroine          ____ Plot
   ____ Hero             ____ Inspirational theme
   ____ Setting          ____ Secondary characters

5. These characters were special because? _____
_____
_____

6. How has this book inspired your life? _____
_____
_____

7. What settings would you like to see covered in future
   **Heartsong Presents** books? _____
_____
_____

8. What are some inspirational themes you would like to see
   treated in future books? _____
_____
_____

9. Would you be interested in reading other **Heartsong
   Presents** titles?  ❏ Yes  ❏ No

10. Please check your age range:
    ❏ Under 18          ❏ 18-24
    ❏ 25-34             ❏ 35-45
    ❏ 46-55             ❏ Over 55

Name _____
Occupation _____
Address _____
City, State, Zip _____
E-mail _____

## HEARTSONG
## PRESENTS

# If you love Christian romance...

$10.$^{99}$

You'll love Heartsong Presents' inspiring and faith-filled romances by today's very best Christian authors...Wanda E. Brunstetter, Mary Connealy, Susan Page Davis, Cathy Marie Hake, and Joyce Livingston, to mention a few!

When you join Heartsong Presents, you'll enjoy four brand-new, mass-market, 176-page books—two contemporary and two historical—that will build you up in your faith when you discover God's role in every relationship you read about!

Mass Market 176 Pages

Imagine...four new romances every four weeks—with men and women like you who long to meet the one God has chosen as the love of their lives...all for the low price of $10.99 postpaid.

To join, simply visit www.heartsong presents.com or complete the coupon below and mail it to the address provided.

# YES! Sign me up for Heartsong!

**NEW MEMBERSHIPS WILL BE SHIPPED IMMEDIATELY!**
**Send no money now.** We'll bill you only $10.99 postpaid with your first shipment of four books. Or for faster action, call 1-740-922-7280.

NAME _____

ADDRESS_____

CITY_____ STATE _____ ZIP _____

**MAIL TO: HEARTSONG PRESENTS, P.O. Box 721, Uhrichsville, Ohio 44683**
**or sign up at WWW.HEARTSONGPRESENTS.COM**